MOON KISSED

CHOSEN VAMPIRE SLAYER

MILA YOUNG

JORDAN CROW

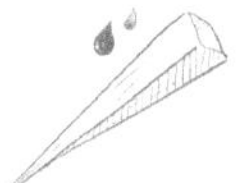

"Wait." Veronica stopped me with her hands on my chest. She tossed her hair back, out of her eyes, and stared at me in what she must have thought was a serious, no-nonsense way. "We can't do this right now."

"Little late for that." I bent my head and kissed each of her rosy nipples. They stiffened against my mouth. Fuck I'd missed her so much. "Your body agrees."

She sucked in a sharp breath. "I mean it, Seth. Now is not the time or place."

I glanced up from between her breasts. "I hate to break it to you gorgeous, but it never will be. You're not exactly dealing with the kid next door here."

CONTENTS

Chosen Vampire Slayer   vii
MOON KISSED   ix

Prologue   1
Chapter 1   11
Chapter 2   22
Chapter 3   35
Chapter 4   47
Chapter 5   56
Chapter 6   66
Chapter 7   76
Chapter 8   87
Chapter 9   96
Chapter 10   106
Chapter 11   120
Chapter 12   130
Chapter 13   142
Chapter 14   152
Chapter 15   162
Chapter 16   170
Chapter 17   179
Chapter 18   190
Chapter 19   200
Chapter 20   211
Chapter 21   219
Chapter 22   230
Chapter 23   239
Chapter 24   243
Chapter 25   253

Blood Kissed   267
Savage Sector   269
Books By Mila Young   271
About Mila Young   275

CHOSEN VAMPIRE SLAYER

Night Kissed
Moon Kissed
Blood Kissed

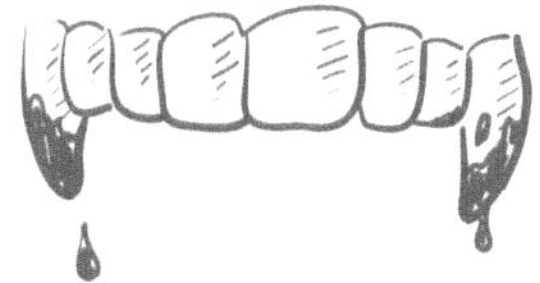

There's a war on...
   ...and we're on the losing side.

But that's not the only problem I've got. Someone or something is killing off the humans in Anchorage... and the fallout is landing right on our shoulders.

Or at least on those of us left.

Seth has vanished. I refuse to believe he's gone for good. I won't. If I have to go through heaven and hell to find him, that's just what I'll do. I owe him that.

And I'm on it as hot and heavy as the growing attraction between me and the monsters I've fallen for. Which is more than complicated. And could use some of my time...

But I've got none.

Another monster, one hidden in the shadows, is making it his business to get in my way. Which means the boys and I have our hands full just surviving another day. And things are only getting worse.

There's something coming for me, and it won't stop until I'm dead.

PROLOGUE

SETH

I woke with my back to hard stone, the acidic air all but singeing the skin on my face. The first thing I felt, on pure instinct, was elation. That burning smell meant only one thing to me. I was finally back home.

Or so I thought. After opening my eyes and getting to my feet, brushing the dust off my clothes, I realized a few things. One, it was still frigidly cold—my breath steamed at every exhale. And two, the light was a matching, frozen blue. Nothing like the shimmering red heat of my regular domain. I looked around at the vaulted, heavily shadowed walls. Vague silhouettes, specked with pinpricks that could've been eyes, skittered through the darkness.

"Shit." I ran a hand over my face. "Looks like I'm not home after all." The cold seeped through my clothes like water. I could already feel it battling with the heat in my veins. "I gotta get out of here."

The last thing I remember was being shackled to the wall by those mother-fucking Seattle vampires. It wasn't an easy thing to admit defeat against the fanged bastards, but they overpowered me with sheer numbers. Add to that the iron fetters they used were no ordinary handcuffs. I felt their magic the moment they snapped around my wrists, a spell that had me literally burning up to the point of combustion. It takes a hell of a lot more to kill a demon like me, but they did what they'd intended. Got me out of their way. So, where in the fuck was I now?

Great blue-gray slabs of stone stretched up to a cavernous ceiling that I couldn't quite see. I kicked at the ground, tossing up little clouds of ice and dirt. Every sound produced an echo. If I stayed perfectly still, it seemed even my heartbeat reverberated.

The whole damn place made me paranoid. The dark was so deep that determining a direction was more or less impossible, except for faint traces of some cold, ethereal glow. When I moved to take a step, my skin crackled, and I realized a thin coating of ice crystals had already begun to form. The implication was clear, and I didn't like it.

Time to move or be frozen forever.

As I walked forward into a looming abyss, my vision began to adjust very slowly. Still, I almost missed the first moving shape that darted across my path. The sensation of eyes on me grew heavy, a nearly tangible weight. With each blink, I imagined these unseen enemies inching closer. Waiting for the perfect opportunity to strike.

It wasn't long before they found it. One moment I was heading deeper into the unknown, and the next, the unknown had come to me. The freezing darkness coalesced around my body, ensnaring each limb in its tendrils. I gasped, unable to keep the air in my lungs. A billion tiny pinpricks seemed to perforate my skin. Not enough to wound—just enough to torture. I hissed at the deepening pain swallowing me.

But then the old, familiar fighting instinct welled up, ignited by an ever-smoldering instinct for violence. As a demon born of fire and avarice, the answer to such a brazen attack was simple.

Fight back.

The tide of adrenaline flooded through me, bringing a surge of searing heat. I clenched my hands into rock-hard fists. Steam poured off my skin where that thin veneer of ice had channeled instantly. The dark, indistinct aggressors flinched back from the blazing warmth pouring out from my body, as if it hurt them.

I laughed. "What, are you having second thoughts? Come on! I'll go easy on you this time."

No one was there to tell me how fucking dumb it looked to be taunting sentient shadows as I stood fully entrenched in their realm. Would've been just as smart to antagonize a lion in its den, or a dragon in its lair. But I was nothing if not bold. Wasn't that the reason I had teamed up with a prideful, power-hungry vampire in the first place? Constantly hungry, looking for the next thrill… not to mention he made me an offer I couldn't resist. The thought of Orion, also brought back my last images of Veronica. Of her running toward me while I was tied up to the wall, fear crowded in her eyes. The beautiful slayer worried for me, which was a complete surprise. That memory struck me the hardest… No one truly cared about me without wanting something back, but what I'd seen in her eyes in the warehouse was unadulterated sympathy and care. Where did that come from?

Shaking off the memory that haunted me and made me soft, I refocused on my current problem.

The shadows regrouped, blinking the same brilliant, jewel-like eyes I had seen earlier. Everywhere they touched, a fractal of ice formed and spread. The temperature seemed to be plummeting by the minute. If I let them stall for too much longer, they'd freeze me out. And what a humiliating end that would be.

Long story short, I was the one who lunged for the first strike. The dark, shifting creatures appeared almost incorporeal, but there was something there for my hands to seize upon, and they hissed and warbled in pain at my grasp. It was an eerie cry, uncomfortably distinct from the human screams that were so often music to my ears.

Still, a fight was a fight. I thrived on them and as I tore into the odd, ethereal flesh of an enemy, I realized how badly I'd been itching to do some damage. After all, I had gotten my ass dumped in this forsaken place in the middle of a brawl I wasn't allowed into. This little skirmish, if nothing else, was a good place to offload some simmering aggression.

Then I happened to glance over my shoulder and see a whole advancing platoon of these things, eyes glimmering in the dim light. The skirmish was fast growing into a full-on battle: me against the underlings of darkness. Not that I minded; it was practically a relief to be doing something on my own instead of waiting for Orion to sneer orders down his nose.

The problem was that as their numbers grew, the temperature shrank. Only a few minutes passed before I thought I could feel my eyeballs starting to ice over. Their needly teeth and claws pulled at every inch they could grab, exposing red-hot blood to the air in gouts of blistering vapor.

"Fuck off!" I snarled through gritted teeth. The human oath had no effect, and so I repeated it in every demonic tongue that I knew, building in intensity alongside my frustration. The air had grown thick with a metallic steam. Behind me, a trail of bloodstains gradually lengthened. The pain was nothing. I just didn't appreciate being detained by a bunch of nagging Underworld gremlins.

Another fifty feet of struggle, and my anger hit its boiling point. Throwing back my head, I let out an earthshaking bellow of rage. Jets of white-hot flame erupted from my eyes and mouth. The veins glowed under my skin. All creatures climbing and hanging on to me vanished in smoke and ash, incinerated.

Temporarily free from their burden, I bolted down a dark passage. The wind stabbed into my face and neck, a different, less tolerable kind of pain than the lacerations leaking red drops onto the floor. That deep, bone-piercing ache was the pain that might have scared me if I'd ever chosen to acknowledge things like fear. It gnawed at the sharp edges of my ordinarily unchallenged vitality.

I did not want to admit weakness—of any kind, for any reason.

The cavern yawned on endlessly, as far as I could see, for minutes at a time. Just when I was beginning to think I had either been tricked or would be trapped forever in a barren stone tundra full of things that wanted me dead, an archway rose up out of the shadows. My heart leapt in anticipation. Then I saw there was no doorway beneath.

"What the *fuck?*" I slid to a stop. At my back, the growing ranks of my enemies advanced, but I had momentarily forgotten about them. All that mattered was the door, or lack thereof. "You can't be serious," I muttered to the empty air. "There's got to be a way through."

The wall proved to be both unyielding and so cold I could barely touch it without feeding some of my power through my hands. A closer inspection revealed the outline of a portal, what was undoubtedly supposed to be a way through. I tried everything I could think of to force it open, but the bitter surface just wouldn't give. I beat my fists against the stone, to little avail. A few chips scattered across the ground.

Finally defeated, I let my shoulders slump. The thoughts in my head spun a million miles a minute as I attempted to make some sense of the current predicament. The onslaught behind me continued to mount. I could hear and feel the gap closing between me and that glittering sea of shadows. I closed my eyes and took a deep, sub-zero breath.

Suddenly, a recollection surfaced in my mind. Something angel-boy had said not too long before everything went south. I scowled, trying to remember the words I had carelessly brushed off at the time. Hadn't he tried to pass between the veil from there to somewhere else…and failed?

I groaned. "Don't tell me I'm on his turf now." It was one more annoyance on top of a mountain of others, and yet it made sense the more I considered. That winged, pretty-boy bastard sure did love the cold.

And if I was here, and he was still there, did that mean we could help each other? Maybe. But first, I had to figure out a way to get through. If the sealed doorway was any indication, that was not going to be the kind of simple task I wanted. Not to mention there were some other things left to handle before I could even think about it. A whole horde of them, in fact.

I had to get out of this frozen shithole, and somebody needed to pay.

Plus, the promise Orion had made me of an unfettered dominion over the mortal realm tantalized me even now. Whether or not the vamp could deliver remained to be seen, but on the off chance he came through, I wasn't about to miss the chance.

And hey, if I found myself back on the mortal side, maybe I'd get another taste of the sweet little pet slayer, maybe try to understand why she looked at me like it pained her to lose me. I licked my lips.

I took another breath, held it for a second, and let it out in a plume of white vapor. Lifting my head, I turned back the way I'd come, toward an oncoming storm of darkness. The shadows surged forward. I cracked my knuckles and grinned.

"All right, you fuckers. Bring it on. I got places to be."

CHAPTER 1

VERONICA

The rain poured down in sheets from a concrete sky, filling my long-term suite at the Anchorage Grand Hotel with the soothing din of a storm. I lay on my stomach atop the bedspread, head resting on folded arms, staring out the water-blurred window. Evidence of my latest efforts to study littered every surface of the room, from the made-up king bed to the table beside the TV.

Deep down, I knew I had to put my nose to the academic grindstone. The dates of my deferred midterms were fast approaching. And I really did feel the pressure on the rare occasions I could spare a few minutes to think about them. But in the wake of the time I had spent in Alaska so far, what with the murders and all, schoolwork seemed low on the list of priorities.

In truth, I'd been struggling to concentrate on anything after the recent events in Alaska, the battle with the Seattle vampire clan, the three men who'd invaded my life, and especially Seth. He'd self-combusted! That image still remained imprinted on my brain and left me shaken. While Orion insisted he'd work on finding the demon, I had so many questions on where Seth had gone and if he'd even return. Maybe I shouldn't care if he did or didn't.

Except, my chest clenched at the question, and I sighed. Who was I kidding? I cared too damn much, and since when did I worry so much about these men… these monsters who were meant to be my quarry?

Instead, I should've been taking full advantage of these rare quiet nights, and I knew it. Things had changed since Orion had ousted the Seattle faction of vamps and an unknown third party was running rampant in the city. There had been more murders surfacing rapidly, sometimes every day for as much as a week. Many of the corpses were old, frozen under hard-packed drifts of snow, but unquestionable victims of violence. I'd attended every crime scene and tried to listen in on the authorities' conversations, but they were just as clueless as me as to who was killing these humans. Orion and Logan insisted they knew nothing after asking around.

And as the mystery grew, it occupied an increasing amount of space inside my head. No matter how much I tried to focus on my textbooks, which were genuinely fascinating in their own right, I couldn't shake thoughts of the case. It haunted me at all hours of the night and day. It followed me into dreams when I got the opportunity to sleep.

If I wasn't a detective in title yet, I was definitely behaving like a veteran on the force. Dark circles under my eyes, spent coffee cups filling the trash, neck-deep in an investigation that wasn't the reason I'd come to Alaska in the first place.

I also knew Orion thought of me as belonging to him, and only him. I may have been in lust, but I wasn't stupid. The guy had some serious jealousy issues.

And yet, as much as he pissed me off sometimes, I wasn't able to tear myself away or forget how we fought side by side against the Seattle vamps like somehow he considered me an equal.

But I also knew who I was dealing with. Orion was arrogant and dramatic, and his temper could be black as night.

It wasn't just him who affected me so much, either. There was Logan, and there was Seth. I might still be able to pretend it wasn't becoming a part of my identity. Veronica, the slayer and scholar, was turning into the slayer, the scholar, and the…slut craving three men?

"Oh God," I groaned out loud, digging my fingers into my scalp. "Note to self: never think that again." Sighing deeply, I turned my face to the side and went limp, staring blankly out the rain-washed window. The bleak colors of the streetscape outside ran together in a solemn picture. At times like this, I felt alone. Too damn alone.

Maybe I ought to call Lian, go and spend more time with her, stop falling so deep into the darkness that swallowed Anchorage.

The loneliness was a reminder of growing up in this town, when everything seemed perfect. Until the vampire attack in the alleyway that took my mom and dad from me. My chest still tightened, even after all this time.

If that attack had never happened, where would

I be now? Married, maybe still studying, or joining the police force? I doubt it mattered as long as I had my parents back. I drew in a hiccupped breath.

The sound of my vibrating phone jerked me out of that sorrowful lull. I groped blindly for it over the duvet and squinted into the lock screen. The familiar notification of a message from Lian stared back.

Seriously, V. Call me before I send out a search party.

I hadn't talked to her in at least three days. She was too smart not to be getting suspicious. Wracking my brain for an excuse that wouldn't sound totally lame, I swiped to call her. "Please don't answer," I whispered, half into the phone, half to the powers that be.

My appeal didn't work; she answered on the second ring. "There you are. I was starting to think you'd gotten into real trouble." The lighthearted bend of her voice masked an undertone of real concern.

I grimaced, feeling even more like shit. "Trouble? Me? Perish the thought." I sat up and raked the hair out of my face. "No, I'm sorry. Just been real busy trying to wrap up the semester while I have a chance."

"Shoot," she said. "I forgot about that." She paused, and I braced myself. Lian had always been a great master of communication—she only hesitated when she was about to say something I wouldn't like. "Do you want me to call James to come in and back you up for a while? I'm sure he'd do it."

I winced, remembering him from primary school. The guy I'd had a massive crush on and the last face I saw on the sidewalk after my parents and I were ambushed by vampires. He'd always ignored me, which was fine by me as I moved to Seattle shortly after the attack. Years later, Lian had told me he'd gone into the vampire hunting gig to help clean up the streets and trained with Lian's ex, also in the business. Apparently, he'd witnessed my attack and been the one to call the police once the vampires fled.

"I heard he only does jobs if you paid him. With money," I said.

"Come on." She became gently admonishing. "He doesn't hate you, V. I don't know how many times I have to tell you that he was dealing with guilt from not helping you and your parents, but I won't stop until you believe me."

"Ugh." I could picture James so clearly in my

mind, how he sneered at me, even shoved his shoulder into mine each time he walked past at school before the attack. He'd hated me for no reason, so I struggled to believe he'd change his mind because I almost died. Sure, we were kids but I didn't want to bring up more of my past if I could help it. "Don't call him. I'm fine."

"He might come through regardless in the near future," Lian warned tactfully. "If that happens, I'll give you a heads-up."

"I appreciate that."

"Any news? Or are you just up to your eyes in school bullshit?"

"I'll take 'school bullshit' for five hundred, please." I wasn't being completely truthful, but the yawn I stifled at the end of the sentence was authentic. "It's like I don't want to quit on my degree, you know? I just feel like I'm pulling overtime on life. I bet I could sleep for a thousand years."

"What's going on?" I heard the frown in Lian's voice. "They're not hassling you about having to leave, are they? I'd like to think I'm above bribing a school board into giving you a pass for one semester, but let's be real."

I laughed and shook my head. "No, it's not that.

Let's just say I've gotten a little more embroiled in the situation here than I intended to be." Understatement of the century, if not the millennium. And if I had anything to say about it, she'd never find out. How could I expect her to understand my illogical desire for three supernaturals?

"You know you don't have to stay at the hotel if you'd rather be at our house," she said. "You're always welcome here. I bet my parents would be thrilled to see you."

"Me too," I replied sadly. It had been years since I'd seen Mr. and Mrs. Zhao. I missed them with the same intensity as an unwillingly estranged child. But the notion of putting them in danger via my very presence in their lives was unbearable. I was already walking a fine line with Lian. "It's too dangerous, though. I need to stay away. Once this is all over, we'll have a major reunion."

"God, I can't wait for this to be over…whatever 'this' is." Lian spoke with the silent certainty that told me she understood I was keeping secrets, but that she trusted me to reveal them when the time was right. Meanwhile, I sat cross-legged on the bedspread, second-guessing the hell out of myself.

"No kidding," was all I said in the end. "I'll be in

touch the second I've got anything new, okay? Promise."

"Okay. I'll hold you to that. Good luck with your exams, lady. Hopefully the vampires will let you get a good night's sleep soon."

"Actually, could you tell James to ask them for me?" I joked. "That would be great." Then, fearing she'd take me a little too seriously, I backpedaled. "Just kidding. Please do not call him on my behalf."

"I swear I won't," she answered. "Don't worry. Hit those books, girl."

We hung up, and I started the arduous task of pretending to hit the books. Every word on every page blurred together, even my meticulously color-coded notes. Before coming to Anchorage, I had been an exceptional, almost obsessive student. Now I could not get my head in the game.

And unfortunately for me, the distractions did not stop arriving. This time, it was in the form of a soft, distinctive knock on the room door. Out of reflex, I glanced at the window to see if night had fallen. It hadn't quite yet, which was puzzling. Curious, I hopped off the bed and went to peer through the peephole.

His broad-shouldered, imposing build couldn't be disguised well even underneath the bulky ensemble he'd put on in order to venture out before full dark. In the wide lens of the peephole, I picked out dark jeans and a hoodie underneath a long coat. His hands were deep in his pockets, and he had pulled up both hoods as extra protection against any errant sunbeams.

I locked my expression against the urge to groan as I opened the door. "Isn't it a little early for a vampire to be outside?"

"Close the drapes," he demanded. Then he glanced at me, his eyes obscured behind dark glasses. "Are you not pleased to see me?"

"Should I be?" I asked, rolling my eyes and crossed the room to the windows. I knew in the pit of my stomach that having him over was a bad idea. Each time he visited, my body morphed into a desperate teenager, and the struggle between my libido and mind was an unfair match.

The thick hotel curtains swished shut, tossing us both into artificial darkness. Orion watched me, and then, appeased, he began to remove his layers.

"What are you doing here?" Ever since we'd become battle buddies, he made it his business to pop over to my hotel with some reason or another, which of course intrigued me beyond words.

"I have news," he announced. The jacket and

hoodie both came off, and I did my best not to stare at the way his tight black shirt clung to his chest and shoulders. Waves of thick, dark hair framed his handsome face, his intense eyes never leaving mine. It was easy to get lost in his gaze, to forget that this incredibly beautiful man was also a monster. Something I forget easily in his presence. He noticed anyway and reached for me, smiling slightly. "But first, I must ask for a proper greeting."

"Oh? And what does that entail?" *Hell, don't flirt with him.*

He stepped close enough to draw me into his strong embrace. Electricity sparked between us, and let's be real, his body and mine should never touch if I ever intended on holding any semblance of control over it.

Orion studied me for a few moments the way he always did, his piercing metallic eyes roaming over every feature. They lingered on my lips.

Then he suddenly kissed me deeply, and I forgot about every other damn thing in the universe.

I savored every moment of her warmth in my arms, the weight of her body against mine. There was something so tantalizing about the living in general, but particularly Veronica. Her potential was an as-yet unkindled fire, waiting to light within.

"Is that the way you greet everyone you meet?" She kept her hands flat against my chest as if undecided yet on whether she'd push me away or curl her fists around my top and drag me back for another kiss.

"I don't make a habit of visiting others."

Her gaze narrowed, studying me, while the corners of her delicious mouth twitched like they might break into a smile. "Must be serious, if you came all this way before the sun went down." Her perceptions annoyed as much as they impressed me. I liked to be the one in charge, whose authority was never questioned. As clanmaster, I hadn't needed reasons for my actions in a very long time.

To be challenged so boldly, and by her of all people, caused an altogether new type of friction within me. I wanted to quell her impudence as I would any insurgency among my clan. But the thrill of resistance was impossible to deny. I felt her straining against my will, much like she strained against my body.

I was intoxicated by every aspect of this woman. And I loved and hated her for it.

"I'm hardly as fragile as you're implying," I told her now, somewhat brusquely. She bit her lip to keep from smiling, but I saw amusement dash across her exquisite features. "The night is a preference as well as a precautionary measure."

Veronica rolled her eyes. "It is not. I was there when those other vamps turned to dust, remember? I saw it myself." She paused, looking keenly at my face. "Unless you're saying that wouldn't happen to you." Her words turned slightly pointed, sharp with the curiosity I often wished she did not have in quite as much abundance.

I frowned. "Don't treat me like one of your specimens, slayer." My fingers ran upward along the curve of her hip and waist, over the delicate ridges of her spine. How easy it would have been to claim her forever in that deceptively gentle moment. I could've ended her human life with one quick, brutal snap.

Afterward, of course, her body would be mended. She would never feel pain again. Not the way she felt it now.

She arched her brows. "So really, what's going on?" She paused. An odd recognition dawned in her gorgeous pale eyes. "Have you found Seth?"

The frown I wore immediately deepened into a scowl. I thought of the sight of them together at the top of the stairs in my home, cloaked in the smell of intimacy. The urge to chastise her was nearly overwhelming, but at the very last moment I bit my tongue. Seth made me livid, but I never wanted him dead or taken from my side. Despite us clashing at every turn, Seth wore the burden of a wounded past like the rest of us. Him jumping into any fight without thinking was to avoid the pain he carried with him. In battle, emotions are cast aside, and he'd mastered that.

Long ago, Seth's own legion turned on him due to a lie from another demon who sought his rank and position. But Seth being Seth, he fought back as rage overcame him. He took down everyone who betrayed him… friends and even a brother alike. He knew as well as the rest of us that a rat among your crew will be quicker to stab you in the back than your enemy.

Guilt tore him apart for so long, though he'd never show it, and I was sure he buried the memories. This was one of the reasons I picked him to work with me. He wasn't going to betray me if I showed him loyalty, and if I didn't hold back when he pissed me the hell off. He craved someone he could trust again, so I held nothing back.

Plus, I made him a promise, and I sure as fuck was going to keep my word by giving him a new start. And that meant finding where the hell he had vanished to.

"No. He remains missing," I answered.

She studied me. "Right." We locked eyes. I dared her silently to push the issue, a challenge she chose to decline. Instead, she touched her fingers to my lips. "So…the news thing was a cover and you're just here to see me?"

Just as quickly as my temper had risen, it fell in the face of her sensuous charm. "You would be so lucky," I replied. She smiled. "But again, no. I've received word from a credible source that the Seattle clan is withdrawing to regroup and alter their strategy."

She nodded. Her soft, candy-colored curls bounced lightly. "That's why the streets have been so quiet. They're retreating."

"That's right." I spoke with a touch of clannish pride. "It seems their master may have finally bitten off more than he could chew." There were, however, two sides to every coin. Our successful rebuffing of this first onslaught from the south meant that I had effectively bought us time to mount a defense—or a counterattack. But I knew better than to underestimate my enemies. They were capable of learning from their mistakes, of innovating upon new knowledge.

I had every reason to believe that when the Seattle faction returned, we would be facing an entirely different, more potent threat. And *that* was the reason I had come to Veronica's hotel room in the gray glare of twilight. Because of a certain impatient, hardheaded demon, my army was missing a general. Someone had to fill that empty spot until I found Seth.

Unfortunately, there were few who could take his place; in fact, Veronica was the only one who came to mind. I knew she was able to fight like hell. I'd seen it on more than one occasion. Nonetheless, I didn't like having to ask her for help. Given a choice, I would've kept her as a plaything, a sublime trophy. She would be an acolyte, my first thrall in years.

Alas, such a luxury was hardly possible. I could not tolerate the mere possibility of losing a single stone of my territory to those blood-hungry Washington interlopers. That meant my lovely little slayer needed to earn her keep in more utilitarian, less blatantly carnal ways.

"They'll return," I told her. "As soon as they can. And the bastards will be ready to wage war."

"Why do they want Anchorage so badly?" Veronica chuckled to herself. "No offense. It's just…you'd think it would be easier to stick to the contiguous states. They could roll down to Portland, or even into California if they wanted… although it is very sunny and dry there."

I brushed a lock of hair back from her forehead. "History. I have been in the seat of power here for a very long time. My brethren to the south do not approve." The root of the conflict was ravenous greed. For decades, I had watched others yearn to possess my land from afar. The rise and fall of vampire dynasties had taken place beneath my watch, and really greed has no limits. "Of course they want all I have. Envy is a powerful force."

"No kidding." She watched me expectantly. "Okay, so where do I come in?"

The time had come for me to swallow my pride. I knew it was necessary, and yet each word had to be drawn out on its own. How many times in my long, long life had I been forced to bend the knee and ask for aid? Not many, and certainly not of someone like Veronica. The whole situation struck me as vaguely sacrilegious, but I knew I had little choice.

I tried not to grimace as I said the words. "Will you help the clan? The conflict is mounting behind the scenes. Your assistance will benefit us greatly."

Perhaps it was foolish of me to expect a woman of her shrewd intelligence to throw herself upon the chance for selfless concern. She gazed straight into my eyes, the wheels turning behind them. I resisted the powerful compulsion to show my hand by asking her thoughts. If there was a psychological game being played, I needed to have a competitive edge. I said nothing more, and for several moments, neither did she.

Then she asked, "What's in it for me, clanmaster?" Her playful tone matched the subtle smirk on her lips. I felt the heat of her palms pressing into my chest as she leaned closer, yet the sharpness in her gaze came with a warning. She was playing with me, testing the water, but little did she know I never played the mouse in these games. I always did the hunting and won.

"I assume you'll make it worth my while," she whispered, teasing, and I quite enjoyed watching her.

That was when the thought occurred to me that I might be able to have the best of both worlds, in a way. There was no real reason Veronica couldn't work in her official capacity as a fighter alongside the clan, while also serving me in all the ways I desired. And given the patterns established by her past behavior, I had the distinct feeling she wouldn't truly mind, even if she pretended to.

My true aspirations for her had not been

crossed off, only deferred. For now, I could think of a few good ways to keep her satisfied.

I wrapped a hand around the back of her neck gingerly and held her in place as I moved in close. She tensed, well aware that I called her bluff but that I had every intention of taking this all the way.

"Something wrong?" I asked, placating her.

"Do you always assume everything between us comes down to desire?"

My mouth split into a smile, and I adored the way she stared at me with challenge in her eyes.

"I'm never mistaken." I kissed her parted lips, softly at first, and then fiercely. The air left her lungs in a sweet, warm draft. So many other mortals left humanity seeming like a pox upon the earth. But Veronica was—to me—a sort of twisted blessing. She responded hungrily to my embrace, and in the next moments, we fell back on the bed together. She pushed the books off the mattress, and I aided her to clear the bed.

Then I flipped her over, causing a cascade of silky pink locks. She pulled her hair back and grinned at me. "You know, I was talking about money, but if you have other means of payment in mind, I think we could come to an agreement."

In lieu of an answer, I pressed my mouth to her

throat, breathing her in, her delicious scent layered with a sharp smell I couldn't identify. There was something so different about her and I had yet to find out what it was.

Just below the surface of her smooth skin, fresh blood coursed through her veins. I longed to taste it on my tongue, even just barely. The dark, constantly simmering primal lust in the depths of my soul told me to throw all caution to the wind and sink my teeth into her now, while she was vulnerable and unaware. It would have been easy to quell any last-minute struggle she put up. And afterward, she would be mine for eternity.

I nipped at her. Testing the waters. Her taut muscles tensed, but then she relaxed again. She offered no resistance to me sliding off her top and bra, nor did she make any attempt to hide herself. She lay on the bed like a goddess, her bright pink hair spread around her head like a halo, except she had fire inside her.

I let my tongue wander over the pale, rolling curves of her breasts, visiting each rosy nipple, taking them into my mouth. They firmed against my tongue as I flicked them. Her moans drove my own carnal desires, my cock hardening in my pants.

Now was the golden opportunity I had told myself I was waiting for. A quick glance upward told me her eyes were closed. Her body shifted and arched with the rise and fall of pleasure. When I slipped my fingers between her thighs and under her skirt, she gasped and clutched at the bedspread. A shudder of pure anticipation ran beneath my hands.

I imagined stroking her, caressing her, moving inside her until the peak of her climax disguised what she would doubtless consider a great moment of betrayal. Her cries of pain and ecstasy would harmonize as I consumed her life force. But she'd be helpless, utterly powerless to stop my will. And that made me ache with arousal.

She spread her legs the moment I slid my fingers under the elastic of her underwear to find her wet and so ready for me. Her hand sank into my hair, grasping eagerly. I drank in her beauty, her arching body beneath my touch, and I relished every moan, every push of her hips against my hand. Lust sparked in her blue eyes as her hips rose, wanting more of me. I pushed two fingers into her as I leaned in to kiss her shoulder, taking small mock bites until I reached her mouth. She cupped my face, her tongue spearing into my mouth as I drove my fingers into her unrelentingly fast.

I ignited a fire in my little slayer, her breaths racing, her hips rocking back and forth. Fuck she was beautiful. She held my gaze the whole time, never saying a word, but teasing me each time she let out small gasps. Her lips are swollen from our rough kiss, like the ones between her thighs.

I kissed her possessively. Part of me toyed with the idea of ripping the rest of her clothes off, spreading her legs and fucking her until her throat ran raspy from screaming. But I realized this wasn't about me, now was it. I had to show her I could put her first, that somehow she'd crawled into my very soul and while I didn't want to take her by my side with force, I'd first endeavor to win her over.

She belonged to me, and as she lay beside me, her body convulsed and her sweet pussy sucked at my fingers. My cock twitched, aching with need to sink into her.

"Orion," she moaned, and I felt her legs shaking. I stole her orgasmic screams greedily with my mouth, our tongues tangling together, my fingers never stopping until she was completely soaked and satisfied.

She had a unique ability to make me appreciate vitality in a way I hadn't since leaving the ranks of mortal men. Veronica's life fed my restless spirit. I longed to take it from her and bind our souls together forever.

Would she let me? It didn't matter. From the moment she had first come into my sight, I'd staked my claim. As far as I was concerned, this beautiful woman who had come to my city to kill me was now in my possession.

As soon as the Seattle clan was taken care of, I intended to make our arrangement official—whether Veronica liked it or not. It pained me to admit she could still be unwilling, but her turning into a vampire was non-negotiable, even if she didn't know it yet.

The truth was, I refused to exist without her by my side. And I was going to do everything in my power to ensure that I didn't have to.

For all his aggression, Orion was a generous lover—and he knew exactly what he was doing. I lay in his arms for a long time after we had finished, too blissed-out on endorphins to do much other than bask in the afterglow. He held me close, which was nice except for the fact that if I let myself think about it too much, it was easy to get freaked out about his lack of a real heartbeat.

"I love the way you enjoy yourself," he murmured. His long fingers played along my spine like the keys to a piano. My forensic training told me his fingertips were cooler than they should have been, but I'd come to find it sort of soothing, in a strange, macabre way. Orion was different—

that much was inescapable. I was just getting good at rationalizing those differences in a way that didn't make me look like a hypocrite.

"There's a lot to enjoy," I told him, nuzzling my head against his chest. He laughed and squeezed me a little tighter. I took a deep, slow breath and let it out. "But what about your pleasure?"

"Being with you is all the satisfaction I need."

I half laughed at him. "Hold on, that sounds romantic and so not like you."

"Maybe you just don't know me well enough yet."

Pressing myself against him, I cradled my head to his chest, wanting to somehow believe that Orion was just a normal guy. One could hope.

"How did you end up in the slayer business?" he asked me nonchalantly.

"I guess like most, trauma from death, from losing someone to vampires."

His hold squeezed around me slightly. "Who did you lose, if you don't mind me asking?"

I hesitated at first as I disliked talking about the past at the best of times, but I also appreciated Orion showing interest. "My parents," I answered. "It's why I ended up living in Seattle to move in with my grandma."

He kissed the top of my head and his leg slid over mine, like somehow he tried to wrap me up in his body. There was no instinct to push him away, nothing but settling against him as it had been a long time since someone just held me in their arms with no intention other than care. That confused me because this was Orion I was dealing with.

"Earlier when I said why the Seattle clanmaster was so intent on taking over my Anchorage, I wasn't completely honest," he admitted, which piqued my curiosity.

"Oh, yeah?"

"The asshole killed someone close to me. A new vampire needing guidance, and I foolishly let my guard down, so I missed the clues of the enemy entering my territory. All that bastard left for me was her head." His spoke so quietly, though I still picked up on the uneven tone in his voice, and how much that still affected him.

"Fuck, I'm sorry."

We didn't exchange words for a long moment, even if my mind billowed with questions about who this vampire was and if he had been the one to turn her into a vamp in the first place. And was it wrong of me to feel a thread of jealousy that another woman held his interest so much that it lead to a war between two clans?

"Sometimes when someone close is taken from you so unexpectedly and harshly, all you can use to fill the hole in your soul with is anger, and sometimes even revenge. But that path will not save you in the end."

I wasn't sure what to say as those deep words were not what I expected from Orion, which tells me so much about the hurt he must have felt from losing her. How he still held onto the past, how he struggles to let it go.

Orion's arms loosened around me and he sat up suddenly. He stayed still in the dusky shadows for a few moments, gazing down at me. Then he leaned over and kissed me on the mouth one more time. I pushed up onto my elbow. His strong hand cupped the back of my head, looking down at me like he was about to say something, but he never did. But as he climbed out of bed, I watched him leave my hotel room, something unwelcoming flickered in my chest.

He would've been so perfect if he wasn't my archenemy. I loved his strength, his passion, even his dominance, to an extent. He kept me on my toes, and of course, I couldn't get enough of his body. But as things stood, an emotional involvement with a vampiric clanmaster was the worst idea I'd ever had, to put it lightly.

Recently, I'd found myself facing down an unexpected problem: Maybe there were strings attached after all between us. Or if they hadn't yet attached, maybe the strings were weaving themselves tighter. I had the nagging sense that I was headed for big, big trouble.

"No." I covered my face and groaned. "No, no, no. We're colleagues at *best*. And at worst, one of us is going to kill the other. This absolutely cannot go any further than it already has." Nonetheless, I knew I was beginning to care about him against all of my better judgment, and probably against the better judgment of everyone I had ever known.

Squeezing my eyes shut tight, I tried to conjure up the face Lian would make if I ever told her the whole truth about what had been happening since I came to Alaska. Equal parts bewilderment, annoyance, frustration, and *Are you fucking kidding me, Veronica?* She rarely used a curse word worse than hell, but I bet she'd have some choice expletives for this special occasion.

Nope. I could never tell her—not about this. Not only would she mightily disapprove, Lian also knew too much about what had happened the last time I got too involved with someone. A vampire slayer. That person was my ex, Dylan. And Dylan was dead. I'd told her everything from the beginning when Dylan and I were dating, about him taking out fanged monsters, and him teaching me how to fight vampires. It was at this time when she shared with me that her then boyfriend, also a vampire slayer, knew Dylan well.

It was such a small world. And because Lian and I were both going through something similar, even though we lived in different towns, it somehow normalised it all for us.

All at once with the memory, my pleasant, post-orgasm haze was replaced by crushing sadness and cold, heavy dread. No longer comfortable, I rolled out of the bed and into the bathroom, where the shower waited to help me drown my sorrows. I turned the water up as hot as I could stand it until drafts of steam billowed from the gap in the curtain. Then I stepped into the tub and stood under the scorching jets.

"God, I'm so fucking stupid." I poured a dollop of shampoo in my hand, scrubbing my scalp with more force than necessary. In the wake of Dylan's death, I had struggled to honor him in the way I lived my life. He was the reason for the textbooks strewn about the room. Books Orion and I had unceremoniously shoved onto the floor in the throes of desire.

The heat of shame and guilt almost overpowered the hot water. I rinsed the cloud of suds from my hair, remembering all the time I'd spent languishing alone after his funeral, wondering if he was still connected to me. Now I hoped he didn't.

"One of these days, I'll learn to go five minutes without screwing up my own damn life," I muttered. Which wasn't to say that I regretted getting closer with Orion, because I didn't. At all. I just knew he wasn't good for me, and the deeper I wandered down this particular path, the harder it would be to get out again.

Plus...I felt strangely guilty about him sharing something so close and personal, for opening up to me like I encouraged him to do so.

I had to keep my head straight and focused on finding who or what killed those humans. Add to that list, tracking down Seth. I shouldn't care about him either, but until I knew he was somewhere relatively safe, I doubted I'd stop worrying.

Hell, since when had I grown so weak around monsters anyway?

The problem was that I got along with them too well, enjoyed their company more than I should. I called them monsters, but what if I connected to the same part of them that lay inside me? After all, didn't everyone have darkness inside of them?

My skin was pink by the time I finally stepped out from under the water. A film of vapor coated every surface in the bathroom, and when I opened the door, the steam puffed out into the room air that felt as cold as if it'd come from outside. Shivering, I ran naked across the carpet and dove into the rumpled bed. The sheets smelled like us, and like traces of Orion's cologne. On the nightstand, my phone sat ignored. I felt another pang of guilt as I checked it.

This time, there were no messages from Lian. Granted, it had only been a matter of hours since I'd last talked to her, and she was probably in bed, like a normal person who did not cavort with vampires in the night. But I still briefly debated calling her, just to have someone to talk to. A sounding board for the maelstrom of thoughts and emotions swirling in my head.

Then again, what would I say? *Do you know how to find a demon from Hell who may or may not have transcended the boundaries of time and space? He was with us, but we lost him in the shuffle, and now we don't know where he is. Also, I just had the best orgasm, and it wasn't with a human man.*

"Yeah, that'd go over real well." I sighed and turned on the TV for some background noise. All a confessional would do at this point was get her to call James immediately. And if I thought she was the one who wouldn't understand… Well, the guy who never liked me would judge me to hell and back.

What I wanted was to get on Seth's trail without Lian's help. He was, however, one of the first beings of his kind that I had ever met at all, let alone so personally, and I wasn't sure where to start. Other slayers might know, but it wasn't reasonable to expect them to share data without accusing me of going against the very fabric of slayer ethics.

No. The only two people who could truly be of any use in locating Seth were Orion and Logan. I drew my knees up to my chest under the blankets and frowned, thinking. With Orion insisting he hadn't found anything, maybe it was possible to sway Logan into searching for him beyond this plane of existence.

I just really wanted to know where Seth was, what he was doing, and if he was okay.

Mulling things over, I flipped through the television channels without really seeing what was on. The familiar red and blue flash of police lights on a local news station caught my attention. I stopped there and watched an anchorwoman speak emotionlessly about the discovery of yet more bodies in Anchorage.

"The latest victims were recovered on the inland outskirts of the city, just inside the perimeter of a densely forested area of Chugach State Park. Their identities have yet to be confirmed, but law enforcement says the investigation is ongoing. Anyone with tips or information should contact the Anchorage police."

The report was accompanied by air footage of the enormous, sprawling park, acres upon acres of true wilderness. Looking at the sheer scale made my heart sink down into my stomach. I had decent survival and tracking skills, what with my trusty slayer sense, but tackling an area like Chugach was uncharted territory for me. If there was something lurking in there, it would definitely have the upper hand.

Still, I pulled out my notes and marked the crime scene in the park down as a point of interest anyway as I may find some clues if I search in the vicinity. At the very least, it could function as a reasonable excuse to see Logan again.

"Someone else has to be missing him, right? It's not just me?" Talking to no one was a habit I had picked up as a way of dealing with the mounting trauma that followed Dylan's death. It had morphed from a coping mechanism into a quirk, the method I used for sorting out my jumbled brain. Usually, the one-sided dialogue was comforting, the sound of my own voice a steady hand on my shoulder. But at the moment, it only made me feel even more on my own. Lian had once told me that it was better to be alone, than to be with someone who made you feel alone. I suspected at the time she had been talking about her relationship with her then boyfriend, Trent, but there was a point to be taken from her words.

I shook my head to clear it of all other thoughts. The fact was, Seth remained missing and a killer still remained at large, in my eyes, those were huge problems. If nobody was mobilizing to find a solution, I would. I had an iron will, so there had to be a way. Sitting there on the bed, all wrapped up in the comforter, I began to formulate the skeleton of a plan.

Step one: Talk to Logan—without Orion around.

I liked the house better when it was empty. No heavy footsteps on creaky floorboards, no passive-aggressive slamming of doors. Even though I was more or less on even terms with Orion, his presence always filled the space—and of course, Seth had been a never-ending storm. The serenity left in their absence was a welcome change of pace.

Still, it was odd to think of Seth in past tense only. And it would have been dishonest of me to pretend I never thought of him or wondered where he'd ended up. My assumption had been that the demon's recovery was going to be top priority once Orion's rivals were out of the way. But hours were morphing into days since the end of our last major conflict, and Seth remained conspicuous in his absence.

Given the contentious state of affairs between Orion and Seth pre-disappearance, I supposed the vampire's lack of motivation wasn't a great surprise. He seemed distracted lately with something else.

Every now and then, as my eyes searched for the hidden line of the shore, I thought I saw the withered shape of a hand reaching out from the dense underbrush. The notion that there were corpse bones scattered around Orion's property was more than a paranoid delusion. Sometimes the memories of our most recent victim flashed unbidden through my mind. It was his hand disappearing beneath the broken layer of ice.

But why was he the one who chose to haunt me? There were others—too many to count. In a way, it was my obligation as a guardian, a messenger, a sentinel, to facilitate the transition between the living and the dead. Had I lived a different life, it might have been a romantic duty, a fulfilling role. My own inherent tragedy made such a thing impossible.

I was not the angel who waited with outstretched hands to escort a dying grandmother to her place in the afterlife. I was never allowed the privilege of protecting the souls of the blessed on their way to eternal life. Those like me, who were born of dark and barren sorrow, witnessed unbearable agony and listened to the screams of the damned. When I stepped across dimensions into the mortal plane, I questioned if these banal horrors would follow me through.

So far, they hadn't—until recently.

The visions happened randomly, without any kind of discernible pattern. I'd be walking down the road and see a man in the middle of the street whose face was mashed into a gruesome pile. Once in the morning I had opened my eyes to the sight of a fang-toothed monstrosity with vertical black slits for eyes, wrenching a hole in reality and screaming through. The shrill, piercing sound of its shriek stayed with me for days.

Soon after that, they began to arrive in a steady stream, passing through in a rush of often unintelligible whispers. Most looked relatively normal, betrayed only by vague hints at the nature of their deaths. A young lady with the brutal scarlet lines of strangulation across her throat. A boy with a drowned and bloated face. In the early days, the macabre parade had nearly driven me to madness.

Now, I hardly saw. Even when they seeped into my dreams, I remained ambivalent. I moved through the motions of my day in willful ignorance, because I served another now, at least for the time being. This sudden influx of free time did not signify an openness to becoming a spirit magnet.

But the tide of ghosts seeking attention only swelled, to the point where I felt a surge of strange relief whenever I heard Orion walking through the door. The vampire clanmaster was like a curse to spirits, even angry ones. *Perhaps,* I thought, *they don't like being reminded of what could have been.* The moment Orion entered the vicinity, any phantoms dissipated like wisps of smoke.

It was a quality I rapidly learned to appreciate. But of course, my need for his unique anti-charms came at a time when alone in the house with me was the last place Orion wanted to be. Sometimes we hit the streets together, cleaning up Seattle's last dregs. More often, he struck out alone.

"Stand by," he would say. "You're my backup." The calls for reinforcement rarely reached me.

Not that I really wondered what he was doing as he prowled his own city by night. Orion's nonchalant arrogance tended to blind him to certain details, such as the fact that he was saturated with Veronica's aura after many of his excursions. I could practically taste her on him.

Who does he think he's fooling?

The answer was probably no one. Orion's jealousy made him a boaster. No doubt he wanted me and everyone else in the city to know that he had claimed her as his own. More than once, I fought the rising urge to ask him how she was. I knew he wouldn't like knowing his girl was on anyone else's mind, and the last thing I needed or wanted was to take Seth's place as the mercurial vampire's punching bag.

Orion kept an eye on Veronica. And I kept seeing ghosts. For days at a time, they would escalate from portraits of simple death into portraits of violence and torture. But it wasn't until I started to recognize certain wound patterns that I really paid attention. There was no mistaking the distinctive tearing slashes through necks and stomachs and chest walls. I had seen them before—with Veronica, ironically—at the murder scene in the woods.

A scene Orion had not witnessed. I doubted he knew about those killings at all, or else he would have brought himself along every time thereafter. Nor could he be the killer; the marks indicated a rough, classless hand. Everything Orion did was meant to be a form of art. The clanmaster would never have killed so savagely, like an animal, even at the height of his bloodlust. I couldn't imagine it.

Then again, nor could I imagine the beast that had left those marks upon its victims.

We crossed paths in the upper hallway one midnight, and he stopped to look closely at me.

"Tell me something, Logan," he said. "Are you not immortal?"

I deflected the query with a wry smile. "Spoken like a man who is plotting my demise."

He laughed. "Perish the thought, my friend. You are far too valuable to me." A slight frown shaded his features. "You look…thin, is all. Faded, perhaps?" He shook his head, as if the correct word truly eluded his grasp.

I debated for a moment over whether or not to tell him the truth, and how much. A full confession would certainly arouse suspicion that was bound to turn bitter. Veronica's involvement had to stay a tightly guarded secret in order to avoid civil war. I had no desire to fight, but Orion's possession of her was like nothing I'd seen, even from him.

It piqued my curiosity over what he was up to. He was not a man prone to the whims of love as far as I understood. I had learned to tell when Orion was scheming. And although I couldn't say precisely why, his investment in Veronica reeked of motive.

"The spirits are walking," I told him at length. "Through the house. Is there a graveyard in the cellar that you may have forgotten to warn me about?"

Again, the vampire laughed, showing his gleaming, subtly pointed canines. "Spare me, Logan. I'm not a highly superstitious being, but you won't see me treading on burial grounds, either. The rival clans are more than enough complication for me." As if to emphasize his point, he rolled his eerie, metallic eyes and sighed.

"Well…" I paused. He looked at me expectantly. "They don't like you very much."

He smiled. "Is that so? You can let the spirits know the feeling is mutual." Then he clapped me on the shoulder and brushed by. "Take care of yourself, Logan. My cursed brethren to the south will be back for another fight before we know it. And they will be stronger next time."

I watched his back recede into the shadows. The door to the master bedroom opened and closed, and the lock slid into place. If I'd had a goal in sharing that information, it hadn't been realized. Sometimes there grew a sneaking suspicion in the back of my mind that Orion was playing dumb as a way to maintain the upper hand, conceal the extent of his knowledge.

If so, the tactic was proving to be as effective as he needed, and frustrating as well. I stalked sullenly down the stairs, hands in pockets. Now I was left to ruminate over how much he might already know. Was it possible that Orion *did* know of the anonymous maiming victims spread out around the city?

He wasn't the killer. But could he have orchestrated so many murders? The man had an entire clan of vampires at his disposal, after all.

At the bottom of the staircase, I turned and gazed up at the mouth of the dark, still corridor. The click of the door lock was the last sound Orion had made. Silence reigned, almost louder than my thoughts.

No. The conclusion I had started to come to was preposterous. Why would he have to hide his identity? I had witnessed him killing in the street, making sordid examples of his enemies. As clanmaster, he had the right and the privilege to execute at his discretion, and he did.

The night air embraced me as I stepped onto the porch. I closed my eyes as it ran its thin, frigid fingers through my hair and stretched my power outward. Anchorage teemed with souls, living and dead. I sifted through the city's wild energy, searching for anything that could be considered an anomaly. Anything simmering with rage, hunting for victims, about to explode outward.

And as it had in many nights past, my patient search bore fruit. One of the first things I had learned to recognize as a harbinger of death was the way a mortal soul looked and felt as it prepared to make its transition from one realm to the next. On the outskirts of the city's sprawl, I found what I was looking for. A life on the verge of ending.

In a dense line of trees. Facing down a killer too strong to defy.

Just like all the others.

The barren caverns went on forever, shrouded in shadows so thick I couldn't see beyond them. It was all icy blue rock, and so cold I felt my blood slowly turning to sludge in my veins. All sense of time and distance was lost to me as I trudged toward the next path. There were only two ways to mark my progress: the assholes who leapt into my path every now and then, and the goddamned mirrors.

Ugly fuckers looking for a fight I could deal with no problem. I'd already left a plum-colored trail stretching far into the distance at my back that was punctuated by half-frozen corpses and scattered bones. But the mirrors were what really put me off the place. For starters, a lot of them refused to reflect, no matter how close I stood. I told myself the ice caked over the glass probably had something to do with it—until I walked past the next one and caught my own eye.

After the second time that happened, I'd made up my mind. I had to get the fuck out of this place. That, or find a way to burn it to the ground. A smirk crossed my face as I wondered what it would look like without all the ice. Just a boring cave. An abandoned mine, maybe. So much for the allure of the Underworld.

Still, what it lacked in excitement, the labyrinth of halls made up for in complexity. I had no idea how many times I'd stopped, looked at some frosted rock, and thought, *I've seen that fucking rock before.* As I walked, I kept my head down and contemplated how long it might take for a fire demon to freeze to death.

Then it occurred to me that if I did die in this godforsaken abyss, angel boy would probably be the one in charge of dealing with my soul. Or at least someone who looked kind of like him.

"Oh, fuck that," I muttered under my breath. Suddenly my determination was renewed. A shot of adrenaline sizzled through my veins. I melted the thin layer of ice on my nose with one strong exhale. "This place has to end somewhere."

"Come on, come on…" I grimaced against the stinging temperature. "There's no way in hell I'm dying like this." I paused. "No, really. I'll never hear the end of it."

My one-sided conversation was cut short by a floor-shaking blow to the wall on my left. A small avalanche of rock and ice crumbled from the brand-new hole, out of which poured a swarm of weird little ice gremlins. I didn't have time to count them before they threw themselves headfirst at my body. All I saw were the claws and teeth, outstretched and glittering.

The searing pain on impact surprised me enough that I stumbled backward, narrowly avoiding the drop to one knee. Glancing down, I saw the creatures clinging to me like grotesque little ornaments, their long talons hooked deep into my flesh. They hissed and bared mouthfuls of needly teeth.

"Mind your own damn business!" I grabbed one by the back of its head and pulled it off, ignoring the sting of claws extracting from my skin. It trailed a piercing, squeal in a high, hard arc across the chamber. I grinned as it was transformed into a smear of blackish red on the floor yards away.

"You see that?" I asked the others. A handful more of the little monsters followed their comrade in short order. "That'll be you, right about now!"

At first, tossing them was fun. Therapeutic, in a way. The motion of my arm stretched out my frozen muscles at least on one side, and it was easy to channel my frustration into every throw. Not to mention the satisfaction I got from seeing the floor change color.

But the flood of gremlins from the hole in the wall grew from a steady stream to a rising tide. And I could see bigger things pushing their way through the wall, widening the cracks. The tiny ones had begun to climb up my legs, scratching and biting their way toward bare skin.

I growled and smashed at them with my fists. They fell away with crushed skulls and broken legs. If I took a step, the ground crunched beneath my boot. The scene had gone from 'iced-over catacomb' to 'twisted horror' in the space of a few minutes.

It was not going to get better, as far as I was

concerned. The weight of a much larger hand fell around the bottom of my calf. I caught my breath as claws wound around me, threatening to snap shut in what seemed like it could be a viselike grip.

"Fuck off!" I kicked viciously. The toe of my boot connected with something surprisingly soft and heavy. I turned my head to see a fat, grublike creature squirming on the ground. My boot had cut a crescent-shaped wound in its side, out of which poured a glut of pale, slimy fluid.

"I did not sign up for this," I muttered, clenching my teeth. "Someone tell me how to get out of here!" I hadn't realized I was shouting until I stopped and listened to my own voice reverberating. Momentarily, the horde of monsters attempting to strip my skeleton of flesh paused too. Seeing an opportunity, I grabbed it and ran.

Literally. While all enemies were distracted, I took off down the length of the room, swatting at myself.

Instead of looking back to confirm the exact amount of shit I was in, I looked forward and bent into my run. My arms and legs were covered in all kinds of blood that was already coagulating in ropes from the cold. I felt like I was running through mud up to my knees. My vision blurred at the edges.

"Shit!" I slowed down, gasping. "Shit." It shouldn't have been so difficult, and yet there I was, slowly running down. Just as I forced my way back into a pace resembling a run, something weighty hit me between the shoulder blades. I dropped and rolled, crushing it beneath my weight and pummeling it with my fists.

My shoulders ached. My ribs ached. The open lacerations stung, and the cold air bit at me through a hundred new holes in my clothes. I was running off of survival instinct more than energy by then. It was like my fuel source had been sapped.

"Come on," I hissed again through gritted teeth. "Give me something!" With a painful burst of strength, I propelled forward, back into a run. The open maw of a doorway loomed suddenly out of the shadows. It came up so fast I nearly smashed into the door itself, but I didn't even care. Slipping through to the other side, I braced my shoulder against the massive slab of stone and shoved it into place.

Then I sank down onto the floor.

The first thing I noticed after my lungs stopped

screaming was that the air in this chamber was significantly warmer. Compared to the wasteland I had trudged through for who the hell knew how long, the blazing torches might as well have been dripping pools of lava. I relaxed, leaned my head back on the door, and shut my eyes for a while.

"Screw it," I whispered. "Screw everything about this."

Slowly, the sensation crept back into my extremities. "From here on out, it's all forward, baby."

Immediately after saying that, I wished I could take it back. The room appeared long and narrow, and one side was adorned with a cluster of five mirrors. They were arranged in the shape of a diamond, the four smaller encircling one large, round center mirror.

I squinted at them from where I sat, unwilling to end my rest just yet. The steady, blazing glow of the torches lit the glass in reds and oranges, washing its surface with fiery colors. I couldn't tell if I was looking at my face or not. It was this uncertainty that finally forced me to my feet.

"I can already tell this is going to be some bull-shit," I grumbled. Upon closer inspection, I saw that each mirror showed something different.

Only one was clouded over. Three of the others showed still house interiors. I studied them for a minute or two. "Why the fuck do I…?" My face morphed into a mask of confusion. "That's the house."

It had to be the house. I recognized the stuck-up furniture, the useless paintings on the walls. And it was perfectly lifeless, as usual. No sign of Orion or Logan at all. "Maybe they've got a search party out for me," I said. Then I laughed. "Nah."

As I stood there looking into the glass, a fleeting, curious notion crossed my mind. "Hey, maybe…" I stepped forward, reaching out almost unconsciously until my fingertips touched the surface. It rippled. My hand began to sink in. "That's what I'm talking about!" The way out I'd been looking for had presented itself at last.

But before I could take advantage, the big mirror in the middle caught my attention as it shifted into motion. My eyes moved to the image cascading across the glass. A forest path flanked by huge, dark trees, gnarled roots reaching across the forest floor. Trees and ground both flew past under the view, which was traveling fast. Every stride caused the camera to bob as though attached to the head of a galloping creature.

I took a step closer, leaning down. The picture veered off to the side, taking a jarring plunge through the tree line. There was no sound, but I could almost feel the thin, whiplike branches and rough brush cutting into skin. But whoever was moving so fast did not stop.

Not until a tiny, claustrophobic clearing came into view. There was only one path in or out, and it was massively overgrown, to the point of near-invisibility. Briefly, the image went dark. As it cleared again, I saw a lone figure standing in the center of this clearing.

A human man, obviously lost and disoriented. There was no time for anything more than the barest glimpse of his face as the picture crept up behind him.

At the last possible moment, he turned around. His expression went from shock to horror, just before huge, long hands with brutal claws for fingers plunged into his chest. He gasped. Gurgled a little. Red began to seep out around the fingers still firmly planted deep into his torso. Then the lifeless body slumped to the ground, leaving that pair of enormous, monstrous hands in plain sight, bloodied halfway up the wrist.

The unseen killer let out a noise that was a

haunting mixture between a howl and a roar. It made the hair on the back of my neck stand on end.

"Well, I'll be damned," I said to the image in the mirror. "Who the hell are you?"

CHAPTER 6

VERONICA

I glanced over my shoulder at the bathroom door as I flicked the switch on my police scanner. An initial burst of static crackled out of the speaker, and I inhaled sharply, jerking the volume dial down. "Shit." With one eye still on the closed door, I fiddled with the tuning bar until the low, measured murmur of voices broke through.

In the bathroom, the shower went on, and I breathed a sigh of relief. It was a small miracle he hadn't insisted we shower together. Mostly because I had things I wanted to do, but also because I didn't trust myself to be able to say no to anything he wanted. It was a big enough struggle to think of something other than his body under the water.

This was the third night in a row that he had stayed over in my room at the hotel, and to be honest, I was starting to get a little claustrophobic. We had spent almost every minute of the last seventy-two hours attached to each other, often literally. It shouldn't have come as any surprise to learn that vampires came with raging, voracious libidos. Orion would've kept me in bed all the time if I let him.

Sitting down in the chair, I scooted close to the desktop and bent my head to hear the scanner. The tired voices of third-shift Anchorage patrol cops mumbled out routine updates.

I held my breath, waiting for something big. It had been three days since I'd had the chance to tap into the Anchorage cop scene, and I couldn't shake the sense of guilt that I'd been slipping off my duties. The more time I spent with Orion, the more my priorities seemed to change. What if I missed something critical that ended up putting Lian or someone else in danger?

I needed to get my head back on straight. And maybe that meant asking Orion what his deal was. Ever since the Seattle vamps started clearing out, he'd become increasingly possessive and jealous of me. He didn't like when I went out without him, or for me to get an assignment from anyone other than him. The only slayer work I did that he approved of was rounding up stragglers who were on their way out of town. And he was almost always there, lurking in the shadows.

It was starting to make me uncomfortable.

Don't get me wrong—I actually did enjoy being with him, but I was used to being a free agent, physically and emotionally. I'd spent years telling myself there wasn't time or space to be catching feelings. Especially not for the master of a vampire clan who might have just gotten himself embroiled neck deep in a turf war.

And yet there I was, playing boyfriend-girlfriend with him. I imagined him coming out of the bathroom in a few minutes, naked from the waist up, wrapping his arm around me and kissing me on the neck. Just the thought of it put butterflies in my stomach. But I also knew he'd hold me a little too tight, his grasp a little too demanding.

"408 calling in a flag-down out at 46th and Fairchild."

I snapped to attention, my shallower worries shifting into the background. This was the most exciting thing I'd heard on the scanner so far. Odds were that some tourist had broken down on the side of the road and needed help, but something in my gut told me that flagging down a cop in the middle of the night was more likely to mean trouble than usual.

Dispatch came through. "10-4, 408, can you clarify? Do you need assistance?"

A few seconds of tense silence slipped by. Then the reply, "Motorist is reporting a possible 11-29 in the woods just north of Sixmile Lake. We're investigating. Can you run this guy's plate for me?"

The code made my heartbeat kick into overdrive. One of the first things I had done upon arrival in Anchorage was refamiliarize myself with the local police lingo, including their incident codes. 11-29 was one I had made sure to etch into my memory—dead on arrival.

"Another one," I whispered.

"Sure thing," dispatch was saying. "Go ahead."

More than anything in the moment, I wanted to hear that plate number, just in case. Did I think a homicidal, slash-wound-inflicting monster was just casually driving around at night, looking for authorities to alert of its presence? Not really. But weird shit was happening all over Anchorage. For all I knew, this could be just a regular human serial killer thinking he'd outsmart the cops.

What a fucked-up thought that was, *just a regular serial killer*. But hey, Ted Bundy had been regular, hadn't he? More information was always better. And if it *was* a serial killer, I could sleep easy leaving it in the hands of the Anchorage police. Static cut across the radio and I groaned. It had been doing this lately, but I waited, and when it finally faded away, so had the conversation. Hell.

I turned off the scanner and put it back into place on the desk for now.

The bathroom door opened in a flood of hot steam. He didn't say anything, but I could feel his presence coming up behind me as surely as if he'd called my name. Standing over my chair, he pulled my hair back off my neck and kissed the soft skin below my ear. I shivered. His lips turned upward.

"I was rather expecting you to join me," he remarked. Despite the nonchalance of his tone, I detected an edge of displeasure underneath his words.

I laughed it off. "If I spent all my time in the shower with you, I'd never get anything else done. You know they actually do want me to take these tests at some point, right?" In fact, I had several emails currently in my inbox asking me to confirm final test dates for the exams I had deferred.

Orion frowned. "Why should you need to provide such arbitrary proof of your intelligence? Haven't you demonstrated an adequate level of skill?"

"Spoken like a true centuries-old vampire lord," I replied. "In case you haven't noticed, my college professors don't give out credit for unsanctioned field work. And somehow I doubt they'd be comfortable including me killing werewolves in the accepted curriculum."

His frown deepened. "Werewolves? In Anchorage? Do you know something I don't?"

I rolled my eyes. "No. You know what I mean." Actually, I had almost said 'killing vampires' instead of werewolves, and managed to catch myself at the last minute, so I really hoped he didn't know what I meant. Then I glanced at him. "*Are* there werewolves here?" Now that I thought about it, an angry beast shifter could account for the mauling wounds on the mystery corpses. Was it possible one of the bear shifter tribe decided to stay behind?

"There were," Orion said. "A long time ago." He smiled cryptically, an expression that I took to mean he had personally eradicated the population, or at least had a hand in it.

"But not anymore," I prodded.

It was almost a step too far. He looked at me sharply, his eyes narrowing. "Not as far as I know." His gaze flicked to the open book in front of me. "Is this on one of your tests?"

"It's cute that you think vampires are the only things I like to kill," I said acidly, wondering if he was in rare form tonight, or if this was just the way things were with him. Because if he didn't learn to lay off at least a little, we were going to have to have a talk. And I didn't need to be told how he'd feel about that.

Orion kept his eyes on me for a long time. I turned away from him, but I could feel his gaze boring a hole through the back of my head. Not for the first time, I secretly hoped I wasn't in over my head with him. To be cared about so intensely was nice—to be obsessed over, not so much.

"I'm leaving," he announced at length. "The clan has business to attend to."

"Okay." I barely looked up. "Should I not wait up for you, then?" The question came out with more of a bite than I intended, and I pursed my lips. *All right, Veronica, maybe don't send your vampire boyfriend into a frothing rage.*

"You should," Orion answered. "But you don't have to." He turned the chair around and pulled me to my feet, gripping my chin in his hand as he kissed me hard. I bit back a moan. Literally all he had to do was touch me, and I was falling all over him. "Soon you'll come back to my home," he murmured. "To be with me. There's no need to stay here."

I shook my head. "Thanks, but I'll stay where I am." I knew better than to rush into cohabitating with him, no matter how alluring he could be. And there was no way to explain a change of residence to Lian, who was still very generously footing my bill. The thought reminded me that I owed her a call yet again, and the old guilt settled in my stomach. "Don't let me keep you, Orion," I said, letting him go.

He kissed me one more time. "You are delightful, but endlessly frustrating." Real irritation smoldered on his face, but he backed up and left, closing the door softly. I listened for his footsteps to recede down the hall before I went back to the desk.

"Of course he's crazy," I muttered to no one. "I

know how they are. What the hell did I expect?" The wisest thing to do would have been to get the fuck away from him while I still could. But even as I flicked the police scanner back on and turned the volume up to see if I could catch more information on the dead person, I understood in my soul that it wasn't going to happen.

Against my better judgment, I'd already gotten addicted to his body, his voice, the feel of his hands on me. Wherever the point of no return had been, I feared I was long past it.

I almost didn't expect Orion to return that night. But he did; I felt him slip into the bed beside me. His hands were startlingly warm as he wrapped his arms around my body from behind. A sure sign that he had eaten recently.

Half asleep, I tried not to think about that too much. Facing the truth of Orion's nature was the most difficult part for me, and I wasn't very good at it. I leaned back into his chest and let my eyes close again. He gave me a little squeeze.

See? He can be sweet when he wants to be.

My dreams were murky and indistinct, dark shapes floating in a misty world of shadows. Muffled voices called out to me from somewhere beyond, over great expanses of space. If I looked down at my feet, I could see a line where the ground changed from dirt and grass to icy gray rock.

And if I looked up again, I saw a figure standing in the distance, facing me. The face had no distinguishable features, but I swore I recognized him somehow, just like I knew instinctively he was a man. One of his hands lifted from his side, reaching in my direction.

I tried to take a step. The world began to tremble. I took another. It began to crack. And just as the ground gave out beneath me, before I tipped forward into a yawning abyss, the fog around that mysterious man cleared for half a second and I saw, clear as day, who it was.

In the dream, I gasped. "Seth!"

There were many ways in which I had always been my own worst enemy. Perhaps chief among these was the way in which I selected those who would become my thralls. As a younger vampire, the prospect of turning someone had heated the borrowed blood in my veins. I wanted nothing so much as to amass private ranks of devotees.

Well, the hubris of youth soon revealed itself, and by the time Veronica entered the scene, my ambitions had massively cooled. I no longer had any delusions about the glamor of thralls, nor any desire to cultivate my own. Instead of the fulfillment I had craved, that path had brought me little more than tragedy.

And I had been perfectly content to reign alone over the clan for generations—until Veronica. Suddenly, that old spark of yearning was rekindled. I needed to possess her in every way possible. I had to make her mine. The craving overwhelmed me most days.

Despite my clan of vampires and countless lovers, it was surprising how alone one could feel. My time as clanmaster had been long and fruitful, but what if I shared the future with someone by my side?

I grew up as an orphan in my human life. I was born in 1437 in Wallachia. I had been abandoned as a newborn and taken in under the wing of the army. On the day I turned twenty-five, the Ottoman empire attacked our land. So many were butchered on both sides, and unfortunately I was one of the casualties slaughtered on the battlefield. Bitter sweet birthday really. But perhaps that day wasn't meant to be my demise as I awakened a creature of the night. Like my first birth, I was alone again with no sign of who had turned me. It was a pattern in my life and I wanted to put an end to it. This was a history I didn't talk about to anyone about… a past that I loathed. I let others believe what they want about my age and past.

Coming back to reality, I walked through a night that was even darker than usual, on account of a thick layer of blue-gray clouds cushioning the stars. I kept all my senses open to the surrounding dark, just in case some overconfident rogue got the idea of a coup in his head. My authority in Anchorage hadn't been tested in quite some time among my own people, but there were always fools and outsiders among us.

The recent upheaval from the Pacific Northwest hadn't helped matters either. And when it came to the Seattle clan, I chose the possibility of eternal death over surrender. The odd coincidence of Veronica's arrival only cemented my determination.

The clan met in a massive, round clearing deep in the forests north of Anchorage, near where Mud River fed into Sixmile Lake. The vampires were already gathering as I drew near; their energy saturated the air between the dense, dark trees. They flitted in and out of shadows, passing unseen along the path toward the gathering point. A soft rush of ethereal voices gathered on the wind.

I paused just outside the border of the clearing to watch my clan assemble. As a result of the lethal clashes between us and the Seattle clan, our numbers had fallen. The emptiness was more apparent than I had expected in the space of the wide, open clearing. I clenched my jaw, nurturing the smoldering coals of resentment in my chest. A loss so significant demanded retribution, and I was going to make sure I reaped my pound of flesh.

The others quieted down as I emerged from the trees. Hundreds of eyes glittered in the dim light. I surveyed them in silence, back and forth across the rapt throng.

"My brothers and sisters." My voice carried effortlessly over the clan. "I have called you here to our sacred grove, on this night, to make an announcement. At the next Convocation of the New Moon, we will be adding one more to our numbers."

A murmur traveled through the crowd. I waited for it to run its course. Then I continued. "It is my hope that this new potential youngblood will be welcomed with every hospitality. I know that one body cannot possibly atone for the losses we have suffered in recent months, but this one displays great potential, should she be accepted into our clan."

The host of upturned faces began nodding.

Their whispers intensified and coalesced into a single voice that rose into the cool, evergreen air.

"As the Clanmaster wills," they murmured reverently. "As the Clanmaster wills."

I smiled. The sound of worship never wore out its welcome.

"That is all in terms of news," I said. "Our enemies continue to retreat further to the south, like rats scurrying back to their nest. They will regroup, and they will come back stronger. We must remain vigilant. Keep your ears to the ground. Watch out for one another." I paused. "This land is ours. It will not be taken from us."

This declaration was met by a rumble of agreement. Then a lone vampire separated herself from the others. I looked down on her slim, hooded figure, skin so pale it seemed to reflect every last bit of light. She turned her face to me and raised her hands.

"Clanmaster Orion, what about the devil that stalks us through the forests?"

I stared at her. "What devil is this?" Instantly, my mind flashed back to Veronica's offhanded mention of werewolves. Could she have known more than she let on?

The vampress glanced back at her friends. "We

do not know its nature," she admitted. "Only that it hunts for flesh and bone. So far, it has taken only mortal humans, but we fear its hunger grows."

I looked to the rest of the clan. "Does your sister speak the truth? Who else has seen her devil? Come forward."

A beat of tension passed. The woman stood very still, eyes fixed upon her kinsmen. One by one, they began to emerge, forming up beside her.

"See, Clanmaster?" She gestured broadly. "The devil seeks us all."

I frowned. This was the first I had heard of any such thing, and for some reason, it irritated me. My people weren't overly prone to superstitions because I was not. I had not trained them to jump at shadows, and they all knew better than to lie to me. Pure logic would suggest that they were telling the truth, this nervous handful of followers.

And again, I thought of werewolves.

"Stay sharp," I told them. "Keep your guard up. If this devil you speak of is a true threat, we will find it, and we will strike it down. You have my word."

"Thank you, Clanmaster." They melted back in with the rest of their brethren, and soon after, the meeting was adjourned. I observed as Anchorage's vampires scattered to the winds. My mind churned. In addition to Veronica's ceaseless presence, I'd acquired another thing to think about.

What do they mean by 'devil'?

And what did Veronica know?

The Grand Hotel was quickly becoming as known to me as the house on the inlet. I would've vastly preferred to keep her at the house instead, but in true Veronica fashion, she refused to move. It was certainly a hurdle, but one I expected to overcome eventually. For now, I'd have to tolerate her whims, rather than the other way around.

The arrangement was unheard of and vaguely insulting. Were she anyone else, I wouldn't have given it a second thought. Veronica, however, had a strange hold on me. I couldn't let her go, even if it meant making concessions I had never imagined.

At this hour, I elected not to trifle with the lobby doors. The light was on in Veronica's window, and as I climbed up the side of the building toward its ledge, I could see her through the glass, still working at her desk. The glow of her laptop screen cast her gorgeous face in an eerie bluish light which did nothing to diminish her beauty.

Just as I reached the window, she stopped and rubbed her eyes. I tapped the glass; she jerked them open again. A look of sardonic amusement crossed her face. She got up and unlocked the window.

"Really?" she said, gripping one hand on the open window and the other on her hip. She wore jeans and a oversized, off the shoulder sweatshirt with a love heart and penguin on it. Rather adorable.

"I see you waited up for me," I answered.

Veronica leaned up and kissed me, then she glanced at the clock. "It's not that late." She moved to sit back down at the desk, but I caught her by the arm. "What?" The mood between us shifted rapidly. Her guard went up.

I didn't like that very much. What did she think she could hide from me? "I want to talk to you about something."

"Okay." Veronica followed me to the bed, but she didn't sit down, and she eyed me warily.

I decided to cut directly to the chase. "The clan

told me they've seen a creature in the forest. They call it a devil, and they say it's killing humans." I studied her closely. "Do you know anything about this? They are afraid it will move on to killing them next."

Veronica furrowed her brow. "Honestly, Seth is the closest thing I know to a devil. You don't think it might be him, do you?"

"Not if I'm lucky," I muttered. "Are you sure? I'm placing a lot of my trust in you, Veronica."

"Well, I appreciate that, but I can't draw a conclusion without more information." She shrugged. "I think if it really was Seth, we would've seen him by now. I don't need to tell you that Anchorage is a dangerous place, Orion. There's all kinds of shit crawling out from under rocks here these days. Maybe some new monster moved in while no one was looking. Maybe it's a serial killer. Normal humans can be monsters too."

That much I already knew. I had the distinct feeling that she was holding back on me yet again, and I had to bite my tongue to keep from commanding her to tell me the truth. The line I walked with Veronica was very, very fine—my desire to turn her successfully gave her more leverage than she would have had otherwise.

"I suppose so." I folded my arms, mimicking the illusion of deep thought. "A human would be little threat. But…" As if struck by a sudden bolt of inspiration, I glanced quickly at her. "Will you attend the next clan meeting with me? I fear the others are correct and this beast's behavior will escalate. We can't afford to make assumptions about our safety when we're all gathering in one place."

Veronica blinked. "You want *me* to come to your clan meeting?"

"Why not?" I asked casually.

"You know why not!" It was her turn to cross her arms. "They'll tear me to shreds if they figure out who I am and what I do."

"Of course not." I touched her face, stroked her cheek. "You'll be with me. No one will touch you."

Some of her trepidation remained. She gazed searchingly into my face. "You're serious about this, aren't you?"

"Why wouldn't I be?" I put my hands on her shoulders. "I promise, within the clan you are perfectly safe. I have never once been defied." After a moment I added, "This is just to ensure the safety of the clan, because I've witnessed your strength. There is no one better."

Veronica sighed and smiled. "Fine. But flattery will only get you so far."

I chuckled. "It's gotten me far enough for now."

And just like that, my makeshift plan had been set into motion. Now that Veronica's presence at the Convocation of the New Moon was all but assured, it was time to move on to the next order of business—preparing her for the turning.

Orion was up to something. I could tell he thought he was being slick, but maybe years of unchallenged power as the master of his clan had made him forget that not all humans are idiots, especially not slayers. He might've had many years on me, but I knew when someone—anyone—had an agenda.

And to be honest, I'd kind of been expecting it. He was about as pure a vampire as I had ever seen, and they didn't exactly reek of integrity. Orion was a slightly different breed than the seedy, shifty creatures prowling the back streets of Seattle, but not even my white-hot attraction to him could fully blind me from the reality of past experience.

He was always going to be working an angle,

and I was a fool if I got blindsided. It was a risk I took every time I fell into his arms.

For all of Orion's faults, he knew how to keep my suspicions at bay. My brain screamed not to trust him, but my heart and body preferred to go along for the ride, so to speak. I fell asleep secure in the choices I had made, if not especially proud. I was starting to think about Orion the way an addict thought about their substance of choice. *This is just for fun. I can quit anytime I want.*

Still, it sucked to wake up alone in the bed, his spot cold and abandoned beside me. I rolled my eyes and flipped over onto my back. "What an asshole." But even as I cursed him out loud, I understood that whatever twisted thing we had was supposed to be the epitome of no-strings-attached. No feelings—and definitely no commitment. How could I be pissed about him ducking out when I already knew we were fundamentally incompatible?

Not to mention I had two other guys waiting in the wings, neither of whom were any better for me.

"Wow," I muttered. "I'm really killing it, aren't I?" The longer I spent staring into the darkness, the further sleep slipped from my mind, until I finally just gave up and got out of bed. There were still a few more hours of night to go, but I resigned myself to bad hotel-room coffee and some study time before the sun came up. As the little coffee machine in the kitchenette gurgled away, I put my hair up in the messiest of messy buns and sat down in front of my books.

"Okay, where was I?" I flipped through pages of highlighted text, searching for the place where I'd left off. The rustling of glossy textbook paper filled the room.

Then I heard something else, a strange, muffled shuffling. I stopped turning pages and glanced reflexively toward the kitchenette. The light was on, and it was obviously empty. Only the coffeemaker made any noise at all. *Am I hallucinating? I wondered wryly. Side effect of fucking a vampire?*

But the sound came again, and this time I recognized it as slow, uneven footsteps. The hair stood up on the back of my neck. It was coming from outside, from the other side of the shut window. I stood up, my books all but forgotten, and crept up to the curtains.

The footsteps grew louder as I neared the window. Very carefully, I inched the drapes open just enough to peer through with one eye. The street below lay bathed in pools of light from the arched lamps along the sidewalk. A lone figure struggled along the pavement, one foot dragging uselessly behind. From my vantage point above, I couldn't see a face.

I replaced the edge of the curtain and closed my eyes, focusing all my senses down onto the sidewalk. There were broken bones and unhealed wounds, but no bloodshed. And no heartbeat, either.

I let out my breath. "So much for studying." Although I had to admit that the thrill of the hunt held way more allure, even in the face of looming exams. *Note to self,* I thought as I threw on some clothes and grabbed my weapons, *you actually do need to schedule those.*

Less than ten minutes later, I stepped out from the entryway of the Grand Hotel and looked both ways up and down the street. The shambling figure had disappeared, but there was no way it could've gone far. Once again, I reached out my slayer senses. A mottled path of energy led erratically out to the corner, then zigzagged down toward a narrow alley.

I took off running, determined to catch up

before anyone saw the guy limping down a city street at night. "Why is it always alleys with these guys?" Yellow lamplight reflected off wet pavement, wavering in puddles as I ran. I rounded the corner of the last building on the block and dove into the alley where the trail disappeared.

A dark, hunched shape stood unsteadily against the back wall. One pale, bony hand had been braced on the side of a huge dumpster, thin fingers hooked over the edge like claws. The figure's clothes hung off its gaunt frame.

I thought I could hear it chewing.

"Hey." My right hand slipped into the pocket of my coat, gripping the staff that lay hidden inside. I hit the button on the end with my thumb, and it sprang to its full length, moonlight glinting off steel. "Break time's over. Let's go."

The figure paused. I didn't like how still it seemed, or that I still couldn't see its face. Then it turned haltingly toward me, wobbling on its bad leg. This close, I could see that the ankle joint had been torn through and was now resting grotesquely on its side.

The right hand clutched the carcass of a large rat. Its feet and tail hung limp. There was no head to speak of.

"Begone, slayer." The face was that of a shriveled old hag, her beady eyes glaring from sunken sockets. Thin, waxy skin stretched across the angles of her skull. Her complexion, sickly white in places, had darkened to purple and blue in others, particularly around the withered lips. "What quarrel do you have with me? I am already close to my end."

"The same as I have with those who left you behind," I told the hag. My grip on the staff tightened. "You don't belong here." I could only assume she had gotten injured in some scuffle and couldn't keep up with her vampire compatriots any longer. And because there was no loyalty among monsters, they had abandoned her.

"Left me behind?" She cackled. Her voice grated, like nails on a chalkboard. "Oh, child. How little you know of this old place." The hag's murky, dark eyes lit with a sudden sinister glow. She smiled and reached out a skeletal hand. "But you've come to kill me. I understand. Perhaps this is truly how my days come to an end."

Acceptance slid behind her dark eyes, almost a gleeful acceptance to escape her fate in this world.

I advanced on her, slowly, keeping one eye on

the outstretched fingers of her hand. "Yes," I said. "It is."

She shifted her weight. The broken ankle dragged over concrete. I was expecting her to grab for me, but not the speed with which she managed to do so. Her fingers grasped onto a fistful of my coat and pulled at me. She smelled like mold and rotting flowers.

"Perhaps I'll take you with me!" she rasped gleefully. "You might find what you're really looking for there, beyond the pale." Her eerily bright eyes narrowed into slits. "Or should I say…whom you're looking for?"

I paused. It was only for a fraction of a second, but no hesitation escaped the hag's deceptively sharp perception. She laughed again, scant frame shaking.

Does she mean Seth? I knew the trickeries of hags, and yet my curiosity was piqued. Could she help me find him before I dispatched her? No, it was too risky. No telling what kind of trouble I'd get into if I dealt with the old witch.

I shook my head. "Sorry, Grandma. One-way trip, and you're going alone." In one swift motion, I pressed the end of my staff to her sternum and prepared to drive it home.

She was too frail to put up more than a token amount of resistance. But her icy fingers circled around my forearm, and she stared into my face as her nails made tiny gouges in my flesh. "So be it, slayer," she said. "I welcome my last breath with open arms. But Death is following you, too. You'll see it soon."

I had seen more than my share of strange shit as a slayer, and I'd heard hundreds of cryptic deathbed comments. This one sent a legitimate chill down my spine, despite the fact that in my time in Anchorage, death had been present at every turn so far. I glanced at the hand clutching onto my arm, at the thin lines of blood running down my skin.

"I'll take my chances," I told her. The sound of her bones cracking underneath the force of my staff seemed to echo in the cramped quarters of the alley. Her eyes went dark and hollow, and her broken body crumbled into a pile of dusty clothing.

I almost didn't notice how that hand maintained its death grip on me. I pried it off, disgusted. The marks from her nails stung in the cold air. By the time the disembodied hand hit the ground, it was stiff and a barren vessel, just like all vampires I eliminate.

I backed the hell out of the alleyway and headed for home. Maybe for the first time in my life, I kind of wished that I'd just run into a regular old vampire. There were stragglers still filtering out of Anchorage, making their way back to Seattle. Why couldn't this have been one of those encounters? Kill it, brush off the vamp blood, go home and study. Easy.

But no. Instead, I had a hundred new thoughts spinning through my mind, and the extra ominous weight of her prediction to carry.

Death is following you too. You'll see it soon.

The idea that I hadn't yet scratched the surface needled at me. I shoved my hands in my pockets and picked up the pace. How much more death could there be?

It was a rhetorical question. I was not eager to find out the answer.

CHAPTER 9

VERONICA

I stayed up for the next sixteen hours with my schoolbooks and police scanner, pretending everything was totally fine. But the vampire hag's last words kept haunting me, and I did not want to know what might happen if I dared to fall asleep and dream. I'd already had one weird vision of Seth, wherever he was. I didn't need another.

All day, the scanner spit out information I had come to think of as routine: burglaries, other thefts, carjackings, minor assaults. Days spent tuned into the crime beat in the city had made me realize just how dicey Anchorage could get on a day-to-day basis. Was it any surprise that such an already chaotic place was teeming with super-naturals?

By afternoon, boredom had temporarily usurped my desire to study. I had my feet tucked up on the edge of the desk chair and was spinning slowly back and forth, hugging my knees, listening to the steady drone of the scanner.

"This is unit 341, reporting discovery of human remains in the northwestern quadrant of Chugach. Repeat, that's 11-29, possible 11-1 in northwest Chugach. Requesting support at the scene."

The officer gave the coordinates of the body, which I scribbled down on the nearest scrap of paper. When I punched them into the GPS on my phone, I was surprised to see how close it was to Glenn Highway, the major route that ran locally through the state. Seemed like a pretty bold place to leave a corpse, given that the others had been buried in the forest under mounds of debris-laden snow.

Then again, maybe the randomness was part of the point. The lack of a discernible pattern had made for a slew of crimes that were proving very difficult to solve. If it was only one perpetrator, I had to hand it to them; even in Alaska, not many got away with a body count half as high.

The sun was slipping down below the horizon as I made my way out to the scene of the latest discovery. I looked at the brightly painted clouds.

The car I had called let me out about a quarter mile from the scene. For half that distance, I followed a trailhead, then slipped off the path for the last six hundred feet. There was a police truck wedged in among the trees, its red and blue light flashing over lines of yellow tape. I hunkered down in a spot behind a large, mossy boulder where I could peek over the top and see the perimeter.

The site was crawling with officers. They scurried around like ants across the forest floor, placing markers down and taking pictures. I picked the CSIs out right away, all decked out in gloves and masks and boots made for handling remains. They came in with a stretcher and carried it down to the shallow gully where the body lay. A moment later, I saw one turn, run up the gentle slope, yank his mask down, and puke into the underbrush.

That told me everything I needed to know. Well, not *everything*, but it sure did substantiate my hunch that these killings were being perpetuated by the same ruthless being. As more and more corpses turned up in all kinds of places—

unearthed from massive, months-old snowdrifts, washing up on the shores of lakes and rivers, found in fields and drainage ditches—I went around to countless similar scenes and watched the same dramas play out.

What struck me the most was the atmosphere in those places and how indescribably bleak and heavy it was. In the beginning, there had been an air of confusion, even intrigue. But now the morgue was nearing full capacity, and good leads were nowhere to be found. The police were sick and tired of tagging and bagging John and Jane Does, most of whom had yet to be identified. They were tired of being summoned to remote areas on the outskirts of Alaskan civilization to comb through someone else's makeshift gravesite.

The frustration was palpable. I couldn't blame them, honestly. This string of unsolved murder cases was fast becoming the longest in state history according to the news, and it showed no signs of letting up. All the crews that came out during the long and often inclement nights looked exhausted. They started slipping up when it came to securing their perimeters. I went from skulking around in the dark to waltzing directly onto the scene after the last cop car pulled away.

It made my job simple as hell, but I did feel for them. The sheer number of bodies overwhelmed the standard police force. Anchorage had always been a dangerous city, but never like this. For now, I enjoyed lax police surveillance, but that was only due to depletion of resources. Recently, I had over-heard officers talking about bringing in the FBI and the Alaska Bureau of Investigation.

When the suits arrived, I'd have to watch my step. There was no telling what they would or wouldn't know about slayers in general—or how they'd feel about me if I were to be discovered. Something told me I couldn't expect to be left alone by federal agents.

To that end, I savored all the uninterrupted quiet time I could get in these grisly locations, somber and lonely as they were. My chances to get a real good look at undisturbed remains were few and far between, but there were always copious amounts of energy left behind, which I used to reconstruct body sites from the ground up.

It was hard, depressing work. After a while, I found myself growing even more desensitized. More than once on my macabre and never-ending tour, I thought about the hag in the alleyway, and what she had said about death. Had this been what she meant, this relentless resurfacing of the dead who were not just dead, but slain?

In a weird way, I kind of hoped so. The necessary numbing of my emotions was something I knew how to take, from years of experience. An angry storm, but one I could weather.

By the time I'd hit my fourth or fifth recovery scene in as many days, I had learned to drift in and out of a trancelike state of rest during downtime; at least, I told myself it was an intentional transition. It might have had more to do with sleep deprivation and lack of proper food than I wanted to admit. But whatever the cause, it gave me a precious opportunity to conserve some of my energy.

And that was what I was doing, my back against a thick, sturdy tree, when I sensed someone approaching from a direction other than the bustling scene behind me. Alarmed, I turned one ear toward the cops. Everything on their end seemed normal—no emergency was being called, no alarm being raised. I furrowed my brow, eyes still lightly closed.

A brisk drought of cool, crisp air washed over me. Then the presence was right there, casting me in its shadow. I opened my eyes, tilted my head up, muscles tensed and poised for a defensive strike. Like a snake, camouflaged but deadly.

Logan looked down at me. His bright blue eyes, gleaming in the dark, could not have been less impressed. "What are you doing?" he asked. His voice was soft, but I flinched.

I put a finger to my lips, indicating the nearby cops with a flick of my head. He glanced briefly in their direction before extending his hand to me. I took it and let him pull me to my feet. My joints were stiff and sore from sitting cross-legged for so long.

"What are *you* doing here?" I whispered, turning the question around on him. "You're going to blow my cover."

He remained completely nonplussed. "I doubt it." Again, his calm gaze moved to the police, and back to me. "They have other things to worry about right now." That much was true, but it wasn't addressing the real heart of my question. He shrugged. "I noticed that something was wrong."

Tilting my head, I eyed him closely. "And what does that mean?"

"It doesn't really concern you," Logan responded bluntly, "but the paths between realms are impassable. Something came here and caused a lot of damage on its way through." He paused. "I think that's what happened to Seth."

My ears perked up. "Have you heard from him?"

"Not him specifically." Logan's eyes gained a faraway, dreamlike expression. "As a matter of fact, I wanted to ask if you might help me retrieve him."

"Yes." I replied instantly, without thinking twice. "I can't really tell if Orion gives a shit, but I do. We can't just leave him stranded. Do you know where he is?"

"I can find out," he murmured. He then fell in beside me, both of us staring out to the cops and watching. There was something comforting having him with me, almost like a partner in crime to bounce theories against. Logan was nothing like Orion or Seth. He carried a softer demeanor in comparison, something I rather enjoyed.

The rest of that night's stakeout crawled by with how slow the investigation and clean up went. Logan, by far the most patient of the three supernaturals I had somehow adopted, stayed with me the whole time, hovering on the edge of the police perimeter. We watched the ambulance depart with the body, lights dark and siren silent.

As the temperature dropped, he wrapped me in his wings to keep me warm.

I tried to keep focus on the problem at hand, but Logan's mention of Seth had my thoughts spinning in a hundred different directions. That, and standing so close to his body was a huge distraction all by itself. Unlike Orion, I could feel him breathing, sense his strong heartbeat at my back. He carried himself with an authority that was quieter than Orion's, but just as absolute.

I kept staring out at the place where the latest set of remains had lain, but all I really wanted to do was turn around and kiss Logan right on his gorgeous mouth, press myself against him, feel his hands on my skin.

Settle down there, V. Take it slow. The logical, non-thirsty side of my brain struggled to prevail. It was a losing battle. Suddenly the prospect of sitting there any longer struck me as completely unbearable. I just wanted to be somewhere quiet with Logan, scheming over how to spring Seth from the ethereal prison he was trapped in, and to bring him back.

We both knew the bodies weren't going anywhere. They could wait a few days.

"Come on." I reached over and took Logan's

hand. "Let's go somewhere private to figure this out."

Logan looked at me, and I thought he might refuse. But then he smiled slightly. I allowed him to lead me deeper into the trees, far away from the lingering contingent of officers. Then he scooped me into his arms.

"Hold on tight," he advised.

The next thing I knew, the ground was dropping away beneath us as we soared up high toward the thick blanket of clouds. Chugach State Park spread out below us like a blanket, fringed by the lights that denoted civilization.

"Wow." I leaned my head back on Logan's shoulder, simultaneously awestruck and a little terrified. He held me close, winging silently on toward the inlet shore.

CHAPTER 10

LOGAN

I had known Veronica would be at the scene of the body in Chugach, although I didn't tell her so. As of late, I'd taken to asking the spirits who turned up at the house where they came from and what they wanted, mostly because the questions got them to stop their constant harassment. That night, I was told about a place off the highway, a corpse left reclining among the gnarled roots of trees.

And about a woman watching from the shadows. A woman with bright pink hair.

Lo and behold, she was there, and now I had her in my arms, pressed against me. Her body soft, her breaths speeding up. I enjoyed the way she felt against me. But when we began the descent to the house and she recognized it from the air, she balked.

"Uh, Logan? We're not going in there, are we?"

"Why not?" I asked. The place was as dark as it had been when I left it. I saw no reason to think we wouldn't be completely alone.

"Well…is Orion home?" She looked down at the house as if she thought he could already hear her—which, knowing him, wouldn't have surprised me all that much. Somewhat apologetically, she added, "You know how he is. I would just really prefer not to make this a whole thing."

"I see." I nodded wisely but didn't stop easing down over the lawn. "Don't worry about it. I can take him."

She sighed. "That's not really what I meant." As soon as her feet touched the grass, she stood up and took a step back. "Listen, Logan. Don't take this personally, okay? I'd love to spend some more time with you. I think you're…" Veronica paused. Her hand had landed on my chest, and she left it there while she chose her words. "I think you're different from the others, and not in a weird way. But I don't want to cause problems between you and Orion."

I chuckled. If being with her meant problems

between me and Orion, I had fully committed to them. "That bridge is mine to cross, if I ever even come to it," I told her. Then I took her hand and kissed the back of her fingers. The grin spreading over her lips left me more determined to spend time with her, to listen to her voice, to discuss anything she wanted.

"He's not in there. Let's go," I reassured her, rather impressed that she worried about Orion and I getting into a fight. It told me she cared a lot more than she admitted… she cared about us both.

Despite obvious doubt, Veronica followed me. She slowed down as we approached the door, but I didn't allow her to stop. The door shut at her back, and she stood nervously in the front entryway. I nudged her toward the kitchen, letting her soak in the weight of the silence around us.

After a few moments, she exhaled, her shoulders dropping. "I guess you're right. Sorry."

"I understand your concern. He's very…interested in you." That was a grave understatement, which she seemed to acknowledge.

"Yeah. Let's not talk about it." She gave a little half-smile. "We have other things to discuss."

My first instinct was to lead her straight up the stairs to be locked into the private sanctity of my bedroom. But while she was there in the house, I had this strange desire to ease her mind, to indulge in some of the human rituals I just barely remembered from a different life.

"Do you want a drink?" I asked. "Or something to eat?" The latter was sort of a bluff—there hadn't been much regular food around since Seth's surprise eviction. He was the perpetually hungry one who had consumed anything other than coffee or tea.

Veronica side-eyed me, still smiling. She knew I was faking it, but apparently decided to humor my good intentions. "I want to say coffee, but I'm going to exercise self-control and ask for water."

"I can make you coffee." I had no idea why I was going to such lengths to accommodate her. Other than her exceptional beauty, she had little right to be so fascinating. But she was, for me, unexpected brightness in a world long composed of grays.

In short, I couldn't help myself. And after she'd gotten a drink and preceded me up the stairs, I couldn't keep my eyes off her, either. Standing out in the open, whipped by Alaskan night air and dampened by fog, it was a little easier to stay stoic and unaffected by her presence. Having the girl sitting on the edge of my mattress, looking at me with her luminous eyes, was a different matter entirely.

But she insisted on talking about Seth, to my mild annoyance. I wanted to find him, too…but not as much as I wanted to kiss her. Then I wanted to push her down into the blankets, strip off her clothes and taste her sweetness with an eager tongue. All the things our first encounter in the woods had not allowed for.

"I think I had a dream about him," she was saying. "It seemed like he might be trapped somewhere." She paused. "We should try to help him."

I should have been gratified to hear those words coming from her. Although I might have framed it less charitably, locating Seth and returning him to the mortal realm was the main reason I had sought her out in the first place. And here she was, giving me the perfect opportunity to advance my agenda without pushing the point.

Instead, I stood by the bed and watched her lips move, examining how they curved to form words when she talked. She was right—Seth did need help. If he could have done the job himself, he would've been back by now. But try as I might, I couldn't focus on anything other than the way the moonlight silvered her skin and ran mercury highlights through her hair.

Veronica cocked her head to the side. "Logan. Hello? Are you listening to me, like at all?" She reached out and took my hand, tugging me toward her. "I know he's not your favorite person in the world, but I'm kinda worried about him. And I feel like Orion's just going to leave him to die as he tells me he'll find him, but I haven't seen any progress." She made a nonspecific gesture with her other hand.

I sat down close to her on the bed. She glanced at me, laced her fingers through mine.

"He might be dead," I said, for no real reason other than possible plausibility.

She pressed her lips into a grim line. "I know."

"Do you?" It was my turn to look at her with an expression other than muted awe.

"Well, no," she admitted. "Not for sure. But in the dream I was *trying* to tell you about, he felt like he was..." She trailed off. "Oh, I don't know. Beyond some kind of veil. That sounds stupid as hell, but you know what I mean."

In fact, I did. The veil to which she referred was the very thing I had been trying to pierce myself. And if the sudden surge of spirits in the house was any indication, it was growing thin as of late. Which might explain why someone like her was suddenly able to see past it. Veronica may have been remarkable, but she was still ultimately human.

I paused. *Wasn't she?*

"What?" She reached out and playfully nudged me in the chest. "You're looking at me like I just sprouted another head."

I had thought I was looking at her like I wanted to kiss her, because I did. I thought about telling her so, but ultimately decided to let actions speak for themselves. She kept that mildly bemused expression right up until our lips met. Then she just melted against me.

The kiss only lasted for a few seconds, but we were both quickly in over our heads. Veronica moaned as I pulled back and stared at me with bare lust in her eyes.

I touched my forehead to hers. "Tell me if this isn't okay."

She grabbed my face, drew me to her again. "Oh, fuck yeah it is."

We barely came up for air after that. Her clothes, and then mine, came off fast, and she seemed desperate for body heat, for skin-to-skin contact. I knew that in this particular scenario, moving together in the unique intimacy of a bedroom, I would struggle to stay in the moment.

For so long, I'd survived by disconnecting from the base of mortal emotion, viewing its peaks and valleys from afar. There was something about Veronica, however, that lured me from the safety of a comfortable distance, right up into the point-blank trenches of pleasure. I focused on the silky planes of her stomach and thighs, her soft curves, the contrast of rosy nipples against white skin.

This time, she was eager, almost frustrated, and I admired how she took what she wanted. There was nothing shy about her. She squirmed impatiently as I kissed her everywhere other than the places she especially wanted to be kissed, and when I finally ventured down between her legs, prying them wider as she laid back on the bed for me, she was already wet with anticipation. Veronica opened herself wide to me, rubbing her fingers over her clit. I breathed in her delicious scent, watching how much she glistened with slick. My cock hardened to the point of pain.

"Please," she said, "I want you so bad, Logan." I stroked her with the back of my finger, and she gasped. The tone of her pleading, more forceful than submissive, aroused me further.

I leaned down and ran my tongue over her, tasted her slowly at first, then deeply. She tossed her head back and thrust her hips against my mouth, her clit rigid against my tongue. The air rushed out of her lungs all at once, only to be drawn back in and released as an uncontrolled, near-feral moan.

"Fuck. Oh, fuck. Don't stop."

I didn't. Her hands moved restlessly in and out of my hair, gripping the bedspread, winding around the posts on the headboard. The rhythm of her body gyrating underneath me was hypnotic and surreal. My tongue found its way deeper, and then so did my fingers. Veronica lifted off the mattress in her ecstasy. If she was saying some-thing, it had moved beyond articulated language. She suddenly screamed, her legs shaking, her body shivering with her orgasm. Fuck, she was beautiful.

She squeezed around me as she fell back to the bed, panting and shuddering. "Oh God. Oh my God. Holy shit." Her hands roamed blindly until they found my face. I kissed her trembling body, making my way up to her mouth.

"I need you inside me," she whispered, once we were face to face.

"Now?" I admired her stamina.

"Right now." She turned me over so she was on top and pushed my knees apart where she kneeled. I leaned back and felt her hands and then her inquisitive, exploring mouth tracing down my chest, licking and kissing me. The sensation of her tongue on me drove all other thoughts from my head. I was barely aware of myself anymore as my heart raced, my balls tightening with an aching need.

Everything about Veronica made me crave her intensely. She climbed up and over my hips, then lowered herself onto me. I hissed as she pushed herself over my cock, the tightness of her walls drove me over the edge. She smirked, loving that she had the upper hand, and she rode me vigorously, hands braced against my chest. Again, she threw her head back, and I joined her dancing rhythm, my hips rising to meet hers, moving faster and faster. My attention locked on the most gorgeous breasts bouncing up and down. I felt her coming intensely from deep inside.

That was what pushed me over the thinnest edge. Resting one hand in the small of her back, I let her grab the other and press my fingers frantically to her clit. Then, rubbing her hard, I bent her back and thrust as far as I could at my own climax.

Veronica's fingers dug into the back of my neck and shoulders. She rode me through the entire tide of her orgasm before collapsing on my chest, her breaths heavy. We were both sheened in sweat, breathless, spent. It was the most intensely physical experience I'd had in a long time. And I wanted more.

"That was amazing." Veronica gently disentangled us, pressing her mouth to the side of my neck. She curled up next to me. I pulled the blanket halfway up her gorgeous, naked body. "I really needed that," she said.

I smiled, liking how well our bodies fit together. "It was my pleasure." I resisted the urge to ask if Orion wasn't taking care of her the way he should. Though unspoken, the thought stayed in my mind. Or maybe it was more about understanding why he had taken to being so obsessed over her lately. She got under my skin, in my nostrils, in my mind.

She smiled into my shoulder. If I hadn't been looking at her in that moment, I might have missed seeing her eyes tracing patterns around the empty room. She said, "Can I ask you a question?"

"Yes." My thumb ran down the path of her spine. I was ready to tell her anything—cosmic secrets, if she wanted them.

She lifted her head. "Who the hell are all these people?" Suddenly, she recoiled, then burst out laughing. "Oh my God."

My eyes, which had drifted closed, snapped open to reveal a host of spirits standing around the bed, observing us. The expressions on their faces varied from delight to disgust. I rolled my eyes, realizing her connection with me had opened her up to the view the dead who lingered, as I did every day. Just as I had on the first bloody murder scene in the woods where I opened up her sight to speak with the dead. "They are just the nosy dead. They can't hurt you."

She was still laughing, half sounding embarrassed, the edge of the blanket drawn up to her eyes. "I think I saw Seth," she told me. "Like, just now. He got out of here *so* fast."

"Huh." I searched the small audience for his distinctive glowering form and didn't find him. "I might've thought he would be into it." It seemed unlike a demon as proud as Seth not to embrace a thing like voyeurism. "Does it bother you?"

"No." She shook her head, raking her vibrant curls out of her face. "I'm just glad I didn't make eye contact with him while you were making me come so hard I almost passed out." A little smirk crossed her lips. "I think he was jealous."

"I'll make sure to apologize in person," I said dryly.

"So they watch you all the time?" she asked.

"You learn to ignore them after a while."

"Still must be strange to know you are never ever alone."

Her words hit very close to home, but there was nothing I could do to change my situation whether I wanted to or not. Maybe I'd become so used to it that it was more of a nuisance.

Veronica hesitated. "I guess this is a weird time to bring it up, but I really do think we need to get him back over here. In the dream I had, he…" She trailed off, staring pensively out the far window. "He seemed like he wasn't doing so well. We need to get him out now that we know for certain where he is."

"He probably wasn't," I agreed. "And probably

still isn't. Demons have specific environments. If he isn't in one where he can thrive, he's in trouble."

"How much trouble?" She chewed her lip. "A lot?"

"Potentially." I shrugged. "The kind of cold in some of those places could put him out for good." This appeared to upset her, her mouth parting, her face slightly losing color, so I tightened my arm around her waist and let her snuggle close. "But we'll find him. And we'll bring him back."

She glanced at me. "I hope so." Neither of us made mention of the brooding vampire, but I thought about him as she fell off to sleep. Did he know, right this moment, that I had his precious slayer in my bed?

I wasn't sure, but the thought of his anger made me smile.

I roamed the dark streets of the city, glaring into the unpleasant brightness of my phone screen. I had meant to comb every last nook and cranny of Anchorage for clan members who were hiding or injured or were simply too pragmatic to do anything other than wait out the storm that had recently passed. But I hadn't been able to reach Veronica in hours, and her conspicuous absence was now consuming my thoughts.

Growling, I shoved the phone into my pocket. None of my messages had merited even a one-word answer from her. The calls I made went to her voicemail, which I doubted she was currently checking. Wherever Veronica had run off to, it was inaccessible to me. I had the needling suspicion that she'd slipped under my radar on purpose.

And that stoked the fires of my fury into a blazing inferno. It was not a secret that I preferred to keep my close associates, especially lovers, on a short leash. Veronica in particular was a prize I wasn't willing to lose. The connection I felt to her was too rare to let go.

Of course, I didn't fully expect a mortal slayer, ages younger than me, to understand her own significance. She needed me to make her into a legacy; without the turning, she'd be more like a cherry blossom, her life beautiful and heartbreakingly brief. I was already determined not to let her fade into a fate as demeaning as obscurity.

But she had churned me into a rage, whether she knew it or not. For reasons I admittedly could not pinpoint, I hadn't expected to ever be ignored by her. Perhaps it was no more than a foolish assumption on my part that she knew my mind, that she would understand the depth and uniqueness of my feelings and respect them.

Foolish, indeed. At the end of the night, she was raw and untaught, a clay figurine ripe for molding. After years of experience with this very scenario, I should have known to lower my expectations until she had a chance to learn, clearly, what they were. But what could I say? I was at least infatuated with her.

I walked until the sky began to lighten in the east, warning of the day about to dawn. Burning inside, I took the next right turn and headed in the general direction of home. The undercurrent of paranoia in my thoughts told me that Veronica was using the sun as a shield, hiding from me in daylight.

While I wrestled with my temper, the phone in my pocket went off. Like a starved and wild animal, I snatched it. Veronica's name titled the message she'd finally sent.

Sorry I was MIA. Working on a case.

I frowned deeply. *Unacceptable. You cannot cut me off that way.*

I didn't cut you off, Orion. I was busy.

My frown stayed put. *Too busy for me?*

At the moment, yes. But I'm here now.

The woman's sheer audacity made me livid, as much as it made me long for her. Immediately, I redirected my course toward the Grand Hotel. I was tired, and I'd be cutting dangerously close to high levels of light exposure, but I had to see her.

I'm on my way. You'd better be there, I wrote.

Once more, she didn't answer. I put the phone away and ran the rest of the distance, buildings and pavement flashing by. Without slowing, I scaled the exterior of the hotel in seconds. Her window was open a crack. I leapt into the room.

"Where were you?" In theory, I understood that the first words out of my mouth to her should not have been a demand. But my emotions were high, unchained. I couldn't remember the last time anyone had had such a profound effect on my state of being. She was the soaring high and crushing low of a potent drug, experienced simultaneously.

Sitting on the bed, she looked at me as if I'd gone insane. "I told you where I was." Her voice was maddeningly calm, undisturbed. "I was out, working a case. You're not the only thing I have to do in Anchorage."

I glowered at her. Something different lingered in the air around her, a foreign strain shot through her aura. "All night? I should never be out of touch with you for so long."

"Is that so?" Veronica put her pen down and closed the book she was reading with a heavy snap. A thrill ran through my bones and raised the hair on the nape of my neck. Electricity crackled in the air the same way it did before a brawl in the street.

If she wanted to fight, I wouldn't hurt her—but it was possible to be merciless without being outright violent.

"Do not ignore me, Veronica. I won't stand for that type of flagrant disrespect." I pulled myself up to my full height so that I towered over her. True to her nature and her vocation, Veronica did not back down.

"And why is that, Orion?" She spat my name as if it were poison on her tongue. "I don't know what's been going on in your head lately, but let me remind you of something. You don't fucking own me. I don't care what you think."

The force behind her words was almost tangible. I stood my ground, but the urge to step back took me by surprise. For the second time since meeting Veronica, I wondered if I had gravely underestimated her. "Forgive me for caring about you," I said acidly. "I need to know where you are."

"Oh, bullshit." She folded her arms. "What you need is to control me, and I really don't have to put up with it. You can get your shit together, or you can get out." To emphasize her point, she nodded toward the window. "Curtain's still open, by the way. And it's getting pretty close to dawn. I'd be careful if I were you."

The realization that she was actually threatening me hit like a point-blank explosion. However defiant I already thought she was, Veronica kept raising the standard. I wanted to grab her and shake out the insubordination. But I also admired her intensely. Her convictions weren't just strong; they were unbreakable.

And I needed her to be willing if she was going to join the clan. Any resistance, no matter how subtle, put her at risk of rejecting the turning, an event which I had seen end in disaster many times. With her, that sort of catastrophic failure simply was not an option, so much so that I was willing to swallow my pride in order to prevent it from happening.

"Fine," I said brusquely. The task of softening my tone required a concentrated effort, but I managed. "I'm sorry. It is unreasonable of me to expect you to allow your freedoms to be curtailed. I'll…be more considerate in the future."

"It's a start." She came over to me, stood on her toes, and pressed her lips to my cheek. "I don't know what other women have let you down in the past, but I'm not going to let you treat me like shit, Orion. I think you're better than that; we wouldn't be standing here like this if I didn't."

"That's fair," I admitted. "I appreciate your—" I stopped talking as that whiff of intrusion struck my senses again. This time, close to her as I was, I recognized it. "You were with Logan." My anger flared again before I had a chance to control it.

"For fuck's sake, Orion." Veronica drew back, scowling. "Listen. First of all, it's none of your business where I spend my time, or who's there with me. Second, you're on thin ice, so you'd better watch your fucking step. We don't have to fuck. We don't even have to be friends. You and I could be on opposite ends of this war that's brewing, easily." Her stony gaze bored straight through me. "If you want me to stick around, you're gonna have to learn to share. That's just the way it is."

Her unvarnished honesty was agonizing. Briefly, I wanted to go back to pacing the streets, scrounging in dismal corners for the dregs of my clan. To be told by the object of my undivided attention that I couldn't be the planet to her moon was a blade that plunged deep.

But I knew what choice had to be made—she'd been cruelly, brutally clear. I could either accept her dalliances with Logan, or I could lose my hold on her forever. And if I thought I'd be able to intimidate her into submission, a reevaluation was in order.

Never in my life had I been put into this position. Somehow, I was the one in the corner, my back against the wall. Trapped by my own all-encompassing desire for the one person who could force me to agree with her, rather than the other way around. I wasn't used to making concessions, especially not to those beneath my power.

Veronica was nothing to me. And yet she was everything. I had allowed myself to be played like an instrument. She had grasped the upper hand, and as yet, I had little recourse.

"No one has ever made such frivolous demands of me," I told her, sounding somewhat sullen. Up to now, there had been no place for resignation in my life. It was an adjustment I resented having to make.

"There's a first time for everything," she responded. "You'll be okay."

I watched her climb back onto the bed and pull her heavy book into her lap. She caught my eye and sighed. "Come over here and stop looking like I locked you out in the rain. All I'm asking is for you not to be so damn selfish, that's all."

Those words stung too, but I could see the

merit in them. She was still a human, and she operated by a moral compass that was stronger than most. When I walked over to her, she made room for me beside her on the mattress. I sat down, and she leaned into my body. Her living warmth was comforting, intoxicating in a way.

I had the fleeting thought that I would miss it.

"Are you ready for the clan meeting?" I asked after a few moments of silence. The meeting was mere days away. I decided not to ask if she had mentioned it to Logan.

Veronica glanced at me. "And here I thought you were going to ask me about my exams," she quipped. "Yes, I'm ready. Whatever that means. But I want to know what you're up to with this. We both know I shouldn't be welcome at a thing like that."

I kissed the exposed skin between her shoulder and collarbone. "It's nothing special. Consider your presence a breaking of the ancient mold. Maybe the landscape of slayer-vampire relations is on the verge of change." The sentiment wasn't truth or lie. Historically, dealings between our people had always been complicated, always in flux. Slayers had been converted. Vampires and others had gone rogue.

There were no hard and fast rules. We existed in a mural of gray areas. But I knew Veronica wasn't convinced by the answer I had given. "You really won't tell me, huh?"

I kissed her again, nipping gently. "There's nothing to tell."

"Uh huh." She stretched against me. My right hand slipped to her breast. "Keep your hands to yourself," she said playfully. "At least for right now. I can't put this stuff off another night."

In keeping with the spirit of compromise, I obliged her request—for a while.

I looked at myself in the mirror, half amused, half quietly uneasy. It wasn't that I looked bad. Far from it; I hadn't had occasion to be this hot in years. I just knew in my goddamn bones that Orion was planning something, and it drove me nuts that I couldn't work out what it was.

His nonspecific denials meant nothing to me. Why else would he be so insistent that I attend? I was familiar enough with vampire clan customs to know that an invitation like that was rare, especially to outsiders. Yeah, sure, maybe I had 'girlfriend privileges' in his eyes, but even then, there was absolutely no way this level of access was unconditional.

But of course, he wouldn't tell me what he was playing at. He thought he was so clever with all the easy denials glossed over by great sex. Maybe Orion didn't fully understand that the afterglow haze never lasted forever. And as soon as the endorphins had faded, I was right back to being suspicious of his motives.

Still, it was just too good an opportunity to pass up; I was sure he knew that, too. And I wasn't scared. If shit hit the fan, I could hold my own—or bail, in a worst-case scenario. Didn't feel good to think he might double-cross me hard enough to make that possible, but I had to be realistic. The truth was, I really had no idea what I was walking into.

Hope for the best, prepare for the worst.

Stepping away from the mirror, I patted myself down for the essentials: phone, keys, money, and ID. My staff was there too, of course, craftily hidden away in a little holster way up on my thigh. The skirt I was wearing was so tight Orion would be able to feel it as soon as he touched me, but I didn't care too much. He was not delusional enough to think I'd be coming to a vampire clan meeting unarmed.

As I gave myself one final glance-over, I walked

to the window and cracked it open. The air that burst in was cool and wet, but it smelled new, like spring. Not two minutes later, a shadow fell across the table underneath the sill.

"That was fast," I said, without looking at him right away. "You haven't microchipped me or anything, have you?" The thought of him putting some kind of tracking device on me had crossed my mind before. I swore to myself that if I ever found him doing bullshit like that, I'd be done.

He gave me a look. His gaze roved over my body, barely disguising his carnal interest. "I don't need to do that." He seemed a little on edge, impatient. Instead of coming all the way into the room, he lingered in the window. His energy felt restless. I wondered if he was worried about how the meeting would go. Or maybe he thought someone was going to fuck up his mysterious plans.

"That is not the answer I wanted," I told him, "but we should get going." Sometimes I cringed at the way he got me talking to him. How could I enforce the "no attachment" rule I knew we needed when I was busy indulging in petty bickering? I motioned for him to go out the way he'd come.

He obliged, but not before pulling me into his

arms and giving me the kind of kiss that might have led to sex right there in the open window if we hadn't had somewhere important to go.

"Tonight is proof of my trust in you," he murmured. "In case that's what this is about." Then he tipped backward out of the window. I closed my eyes, feeling the dizzy rush of the fall, the cold air cutting straight through my clothes. How we ended up right-side-up on the sidewalk, I wasn't sure. Orion set me on my feet.

"I'm guessing that was supposed to prove *my* trust in *you*," I said sardonically. Up over his shoulder, I could see the pane still open. "I'll have you know I did not buy insurance on those books. You'll be getting a collections call from Seattle University if anything happens to them."

"It won't," he answered. "I'd know."

Again, not exactly a comforting answer, but I kept my mouth shut this time. For now, there were bigger fish to fry, and it wouldn't be smart to risk alienating him literally minutes before gaining access to potentially valuable intel. *Business before pleasure, V. Always.*

"Where is this place, anyway?" I asked as we set off down the lamplit road.

"I'm escorting you there so I don't need to tell you," he replied, quirking his lips into a wry smirk.

"Are you going to blindfold me?" The question came out before I really had a chance to assess how it sounded, and realized quickly how easily it could be misconstrued.

His smile widened. "Would you like that?"

I kicked myself. Why did I always lose the ability to think first, *then* speak around him? It was like most of my sense periodically went out the damn window whenever he looked in my general direction. "Very funny," I said now, rolling my eyes. "I'm just asking because I know you like to keep your secrets, that's all."

"Of all the secrets I possess, I think I can spare you one." He reached back and took my hand in his. "Come on. Time won't wait, and the clan doesn't like to either."

Looking back on it, I wasn't able to determine whether he'd cast some kind of spell as soon as he touched me or not. But the entire rest of the journey there was a blur, despite the fact that he had just implied he wasn't keeping secrets from me. As he led me up a lightless path flanked with the densest trees I'd ever seen, I found myself wondering where the hell we actually were.

The forest floor was carpeted thickly with fallen needles that cushioned our steps nearly into soundlessness. I could barely see a foot in front of my face. All I sensed for sure was Orion's hand still holding mine, leading me forward. I had no choice at this point but to trust him completely.

Was that his plan all along? Too late, I realized just how vulnerable he'd made me.

Then the darkness began to give way to a soft, ethereal glow. Started by the sudden illumination, I paused for a second, inadvertently tugging on Orion's hand. He turned back to me, his eyes incandescent in the shadows.

"We're almost there," he said. "There's no backing out anymore." The deep hush of the forest seemed to amplify his words.

I nodded. He led me forward again.

By the time we reached the mouth of the clearing, the light was almost as bright as day. Torches with strange blue flames blazed along the perimeter, casting everything in an eerie, icy glow. One end of the crescent-shaped space held a raised stone platform adorned with what looked like an altar and a tablet inscribed with runes.

In front of the platform, Orion's clan assembled, bathed in the blue torchlight. The way they stared with the same metallic eyes as he had was very cultlike, but I understood at once why he'd instructed me to wear tight, irreverent clothes. Beneath their dark cloaks, the vampires themselves weren't very clothed at all.

For a moment, my thoroughly human brain thought, *Aren't they cold?* Then I remembered, of course they weren't. Because they were all technically dead. And that was what made it all sink in. I took a deep, steadying breath. Orion was right. I had officially reached the point of no return.

He gave me a moment to take everything in, then brought me to a spot a little ways away from the others, which seemed to have been specially prepared for me. I could feel the weight of their eyes boring into me. Nobody said a word, not even a murmur of curiosity.

"Face forward," Orion whispered. "Wait for me to call you." He held my chin in his fingers just long enough to stare into my face himself, and then he turned and approached the platform.

The clearing was absolutely silent. No one coughed—because no one breathed. The only sound was of Orion climbing the steps carved into the side of the platform. He stood there for a moment, surveying his throng of devotees. It was obvious that this was where he was most in his element. The center of attention, being revered by a crowd. Typical vamp shit.

"Brothers and sisters." The note of total authority in his voice made me tingle in a way I both loved and despised. My weak spot for men in power was never more evident anywhere than it was with Orion. "Tonight, I want to make an introduction," he continued. "There is, as promised, someone new among us."

I raised an eyebrow. He'd told them about me already?

He glanced at me. "Her mortal name is inadmissible within our ranks. Henceforth, she will be known only as V."

I kept my poker face flat, but a sudden flood of apprehension welled in my gut. In the interest of not making him suspicious, I'd refrained from peppering Orion with too many questions, and I was beginning to think of that as a tactical error. He was using language that sounded as though we were about to enter into a long-term arrangement.

I had not agreed to anything like that. As much as I could learn by being immersed in the inner sanctum of vamp culture, I knew the longer I stuck around, the more dangerous things could get.

Eventually, something would have to give. The fact that he was ready to throw me into the deep end kind of pissed me off.

But then he was beckoning me to come forward. "Step up, V. Let them see your face."

Silently swearing some form of vengeance, I did as I was told. There were too many of them for me to even think about raising a stink. Orion had effectively backed me into a goddamn corner—and I'd let him! Definitely not my finest moment.

He motioned for me to join him on the platform, where he placed his hand in the bare small of my back and pivoted me to face the clan. That was when I noticed just how large the clearing was, and how the clan's membership didn't fill it. My stomach sank even further. Was the decline in population all casualties from the recent turf wars?

Or was the mysterious Anchorage killer picking vampires off too?

Orion was speaking again, but I didn't hear him over the racing maelstrom of my thoughts. I was too busy trying to recall the details of every crime scene I'd been to since the Seattle contingent retreated. Some of them had been bloody for sure, the snow and ice all splashed dark crimson. But others—

Orion's hand slid around to my hip. His grip tightened. Inhaling sharply, I straightened my posture, gazing straight ahead. If he had asked me a question or expected me to say something, I had no idea what was going to come out of my mouth. All of those hypnotic eyes were trained on me. Yeah, it sure looked like everyone wanted me to talk. I opened my mouth.

In the next instant, I thought the earth had broken open, so loud was the boom reverberating through the clearing. Orion snapped to attention. Another huge crash shook the ground. The vampires began to scatter.

"Get down!" Orion leapt in front of me, shielding everything, including my view, with his body. But he wasn't fast enough to keep me from seeing the giant tree at the back of the grove that had abruptly been reduced to little more than a towering, jagged stump. And in the space where it used to be, a wild, ethereal creature loomed way up into the shadows.

With one long arm, it reached forward and snatched up a fleeing vamp in its taloned fingers. I forced my way around Orion just in time to see that vampire lose his head to jaws made of bleached white bone. The black antlers protruding from either side of the bare skull ended in brutal points.

"What the hell is that thing?" I whispered, awestruck.

Orion grimaced. "Soon," he growled, "it will be dead."

I had made the room with the cluster of mirrors into my unofficial home away from home. The cold still dug its claws into my bones if I stayed too still for too long, but for some reason, as long as I hung out near the mirrors, the other creatures in the Underworld didn't want to bother with me. I could still see them hanging out in the darkness, waiting for me to come out and play.

I did keep an eye on Orion and angel boy through my mirrors. It wasn't them I wanted to see as much as the sexy slayer. I could tell Orion was being surly with her, trying to keep her all to himself, so it gratified me to look in one day and see her and Logan going at it hard while Orion was out of the house.

She might have seen me then, but I didn't really care. If I ever found a way to return, my number one goal was to get her on her back again anyway. From my vantage point in the room full of mirrors, it sure looked like she could use a stress reliever. I'd watched her visit body scene after body scene and struggle to put the murder pieces together.

It was during times like these that her newness and inexperience really showed. She was younger than all of us by generations; the girl had a lot of ground to make up for. And Orion's constant hovering didn't help her do it. Whenever I happened to catch them together, I willed Veronica to haul off and punch him in the face—or the dick. On more than one occasion, she'd looked like she was thinking about it.

I paced around the chamber, trying to get the blood pumping through my veins again. Too much time in the cold made it all feel like mud in there. Everything got sluggish and weird, like I was trapped in an underwater swamp. As I moved, I kept my eye on the mirrors. Veronica and Orion had been active for a while. I'd appreciated her skimpy, racy little outfit until I realized it was all for him.

"Greedy bastard," I muttered to no one. Who the fuck did he think he was, keeping her all to himself? In my opinion, she'd been enjoying herself way more when it was Logan on top of, behind, and underneath her. Obviously Orion wasn't the only one who had carnal needs demanding to be met.

But he was the one dragging her through the forest on some bullshit vampire vision quest. I'd stopped watching as soon as they reached the meeting grounds in the grove. That was a place I knew, and not one I remembered fondly. His fucking race had hated me from day one.

My gaze was somewhere else at the exact moment the shit hit the fan—but I still heard and felt the impact of that tree getting snapped in half like a twig. The scene that immediately followed, of vampires scurrying like roaches under a bright light, gave me an almost visceral satisfaction that was undercut by furious jealousy.

I wanted to be the one turning and fighting that ugly thing, swinging from its antlers as I snapped its neck and lit a literal fire in its skull. Just watching it tear into Orion's precious sycophants made my blood boil with violent glee. He had already sustained considerable losses following the invasion from the south. Part of me hoped this attack would be the last straw, that he and his cult would break and fall apart under the onslaught. I'd be out of a job then, but what did it matter? He'd be too weak to keep me from running amok.

The grin started to slip off my face as the ocean of vamps continued to part and scatter. None of them seemed to be any match for whatever hellspawn had been visited upon them. They fell like paper dolls at its brutally clawed hands. I watched the borrowed life drain from their eyes. More than one head rolled across the clearing after an unceremonious removal from its body.

"Hey!" The shout startled me. Mirroring my reaction, the creature whipped around, searching for the source of the sound. I saw her before it did; her pink cotton-candy hair whirled by. She had a long, thin weapon in her hand, slicing through the air. She brandished it fiercely. Not an ounce of fear showed in her eyes. "Over here, ugly," she called.

The creature moved to focus on her. It

bounded forward, its stride long and loping. A gust of wind blew Veronica's mane of curls across her face, but she didn't flinch. The point of her staff stayed aiming true at her target.

"Veronica!"

I recognized Orion's voice, slightly unhinged from panic and rage. He showed up at the edge of the creature's field of vision, and for a second, I couldn't comprehend his physical form. He had gone full vamp: eyes blazing, fangs jutting from his mouth, bloodless veins raised on his skin. Looking at him, I thought I kind of preferred him that way. He was more authentic, more intimidating. This version of him helped me understand how he'd gotten to be clanmaster.

Veronica, however, was completely unfazed. "Shut up, Orion!" she shot back. "Do you want to get out of here or not?" Her eyes, clearly annoyed, darted to the side. "Either help me take this thing down or get out of the way!"

I had never wanted her more.

Provoked by all the shouting, the creature took a heavy swing at Veronica. She dodged nimbly out of the way, using her staff to deflect the blow. I could see that it was sharpened on one end, almost like an oversized needle. Then the design finally clicked in my head. She was wielding a massive silver stake.

Did Orion have a death wish, or what? No wonder he was so obsessed with her. She walked around with the very thing that could ruin him. Maybe that was what he really wanted to control. As I tracked her leaps and flips around the clearing, I smirked. No matter the size of his engorged ego, he couldn't control *that* if his un-life depended on it.

It was a small consolation that I didn't have to see him for most of the fight. Veronica moved with the grace and strength of a tiger, occasionally darting in like a bullfighter to bleed her quarry. She was lightning-fast, and she had an uncanny clairvoyance toward the creature's next move. Everything it did appeared to be half a second too late.

Only once did Veronica get caught moving too slow, and it cost her a thick lock of her hair. She saw it lying on the ground as she came up from her duck, and her face darkened like an oncoming storm. The next time the creature had the audacity to reach for her, she flourished her staff. One of the bony, pointed fingers fell limply to the dirt.

The creature howled, recoiling. I saw a dark, wine-colored water sprout erupt into existence, joining the rest of the splattered blood. All the thrashing that ensued in the aftermath of an impromptu amputation meant I only caught glimpses of her cocking her arm back, aiming with the point of her staff.

Then the creature's viewpoint was pulled and pinned to the night sky—no doubt held there by Orion. I heard the singing of the staff as it cut through the air. The image in the mirror shook. It grew fuzzy around the edges. I thought she had this thing in the bag.

I was wrong.

The surface of the mirror flashed a sudden, blinding white, so bright I had to look away A piercing roar ripped through the cavern. When I was able to see again, I caught sight of Orion being wrenched from the behemoth's back, crushed in its grasp. The pressure made his eyes widen and turned his skin grayer than usual. In the back-ground, Veronica was screaming.

There was a sickening crack. Orion went too limp too fast. He was tossed aside, out of view. The sound of his body landing made the hair stand up on the back of my neck. Under other circumstances, I might have enjoyed the moment. But if he had just gotten his ass kicked, then Veronica was likely alone. Orion's underlings had already proven their cowardice.

It advanced on her. She was standing, but a patch of dark blood had bloomed on the front of her clothes; whose blood that was, I didn't know. This time, her gaze did not stay steady; she kept trying to steal glances at Orion. Probably thought he was dead as a doornail, like the others. I couldn't really blame her, but I hated that her focus was split. That was a recipe for disaster.

Unless I found a way to help. I turned to Logan's mirror. The glass was dark, inert. Impatient, I knocked hard on the surface, generating silver ripples. An image began to form, but it wasn't clear enough. I could only see him, not where he was or what he was doing.

"Logan!" Again, I knocked on the glass. "Hey, asshole! Can you hear me?" No response. I tried again. "I'm sorry I called you an asshole just now. Orion just got his shit rocked, and Veronica's in trouble. You gotta go help her out!"

He looked up, and I felt a rush of excited adrenaline. But it was something else that caught his eye. I might as well have been shouting at a brick wall.

"Logan, she's gonna die!" I pounded the icy walls with my fist. The mirrors swayed precariously. One mirror over, Veronica parried the creature's strike. But she was getting tired—sooner or later, she'd falter. Normally, I delighted in scenarios of brutality, but I didn't want to think about what would happen to her.

"Logan! You fucking—" I let out a growl of pure frustration. It wasn't working even a little bit. Wherever I'd been locked up, it wasn't the place he could see all the time. "Of course not," I muttered. "Why would it be that fucking easy?"

Stepping back from the wall, I tried to collect myself. The mirrors mocked me. Orion's was pitch black, completely unmoving. Veronica narrowly landed her next block. Her back foot slid on the ground, and I held my breath, waiting to see if she'd fall. Her face contorted from exertion, she managed to force her adversary back.

But it took her too long to get back into fighting position. Her adrenaline high was beginning to wear off. She was exhausted.

My hands balled up into fists so tight the nails drew blood from my palms. Then, suddenly, my field of view swung completely around, past Orion's crumpled body. Someone brand new had come barreling into the clearing. He charged, raising a gleaming, mean-looking blade.

The blue light glinted off its sharpest edge as it came arcing down.

I raced above the tree line, face numbed by the cruel edge of the wind. The agitated chatter of spirits rang in my ears. Minutes ago, they had started to become even more restless than usual, like wild animals before a storm. But I didn't need them to tell me when the impact hit—because Orion and Veronica had both been caught in it. A sour sense of duty propelled me on toward Orion's location.

For Veronica, however, the feeling was much closer to real fear. She was strong, fast, more than capable. But I cared about her so…differently.

As soon as I homed in on the chaotic cluster of energy surrounding her, I knew exactly where they were. Winging my way over the dark mass of the forest, I wondered what Orion's motivation for bringing her to the clearing really was. In all the time I had known him, he'd never opened the clan's meeting grounds to anyone else. Veronica seemed to always be the exception.

But my train of thought was interrupted upon arriving at the grove. From the air, I could see what looked like bodies strewn across the dirt. The massive, broken trunk of a destroyed tree carved a trench where it lay, and in its shadow, two figures squared off. One was a towering monster with claws for fingers and a bare skull for a head, two branching antlers protruding from the bone. The hollows of its eyes glowed with a pale, baleful light.

The other was a human man wielding a long, sharp sword. He had a body slung over his shoulder. Veronica's face was out of sight, but I recognized her hair instantly. One of her arms hung limply over the man's shoulder, but she was still alive—even in the midst of all the white noise, I picked out the faint hum of her energy. The human was saving her from the monster.

The skull-headed monster swayed on its massive hind feet. It was bleeding profusely from a deep wound slashed across the front of its gaunt torso, presumably by the sword in the human's hand. Great drops of black blood splashed onto the forest floor beneath it. The creature's movements were hesitant, unsure. Then the man glanced to the side. The creature lunged as soon as he looked away.

The man's sword jabbed forward, a quick lance of moonlight. I heard the crack of the monster's ribs as clear as a gunshot on a silent night, followed by a hoarse howl of anguish. It recoiled, clutching at the new gash as yet more blood flooded through its fingers.

The man slipped into the trees so quickly and quietly that I might have missed his exit if I hadn't been watching him already. He took both his weapon and Veronica with him, and in little more than a second, he had passed out of sight. I darted after them to the edge of the woods to where they were no longer in sight. Briefly, I could still hear him moving through the foliage, but soon, even that trace of him had faded away.

Just as I was about to abandon the grove that was now a vampire graveyard in favor of tracking Veronica's captor back to wherever he was taking her, I noticed Orion lying motionless in the dirt like so many of his clan members. Like Veronica, however, I felt his energy fighting to stay stable. He was severely injured.

"Shit," I muttered. Although my desire to pursue Veronica hadn't lessened, I understood the man who took her would care for her injuries, and seeing as he protected her, I guessed he was a friend and not enemy an her. I also understood implicitly where my duty lay. She'd been my lover once, my confidante a couple times as well. But he was master of the Anchorage clan, and I'd sworn to help him long before I ever knew Veronica existed.

At the moment, it looked for all the world like Orion was about to die—if he hadn't already. I grimaced and set the angle of my wings into a sharp dive. The grotesque, bleeding, hulking creature pivoted sluggishly in my direction. It ducked as I skimmed low over its head, barely avoiding the jagged points of its antlers.

Maybe that had been a little too close. One wrong pass could ground me for good. Nonetheless, I banked around in a tight curve and dove again. Up close, my target appeared to be in varying states of decay. White bone showed through strings of sinew and the patchy remains of a pelt. When it dodged, the creature wobbled dangerously.

I didn't want it to fall; I wanted it to leave. The last thing I needed was to deal with two potential corpses instead of one. "Come on," I whispered under my breath. "Get out of here."

On the third pass, it tried to swat me out of the air. Rolling nimbly out of the way, I watched the creature teeter nimbly on the very margins of its balance. The ground below was soaked in blood. I sensed the creature weakening little by little. But finally, the self-preservation instinct kicked in. With one last glare from its empty eye sockets, it limped off in the opposite direction of Veronica and the stranger.

I landed next to Orion's body. He was splayed out on his side; as I turned him over, I saw that he had turned an alarming shade of gray. This, I knew, was bad even for him. A vampire couldn't survive dying twice, no matter who he was.

And it certainly looked like Orion was headed that way. His eyes had rolled back in his head, irises barely visible. I propped him up on my lap, supporting his head as it lolled to the side. He would've been furious to know anyone saw him in such condition.

"Hey." I passed my hand in front of his face and shook him gently. "Anyone in there?" No response.

"C'mon, Orion. Time to switch the lights on." With the flat of my hand, I slapped him lightly. Just enough to give him a jumpstart.

Probably the only time I'll ever get away with that, I thought, smirking wryly to myself. But he still lay absolutely motionless in my lap. His shirt and jeans were torn, perhaps by antlers, but I found no obvious wounds—and of course, there was no blood. Had he died of internal trauma already? Was that even possible?

"I thought you guys were supposed to be invincible," I muttered. "Or at least immortal."

He didn't answer. I laid my palm on his chest, took a deep breath, and closed my eyes. If there was nothing to be seen but a void, then we were in real trouble. But somewhere, far down in the depths of swirling shadows that threatened to eclipse him entirely, I saw a little spark of something.

I had been almost too late—but not quite. A river of energy flooded the darkness in which Orion's spirit floundered, bolstering its light and bringing it back from the edge of extinguishing. In a moment, that spark had blossomed into a flame, small but steady.

I opened my eyes, and so did he. He stared at me, briefly unseeing.

"Hello," I said. "You're welcome."

The vampire sat bolt upright. His gaze, suddenly frantic, swept around the ruined grove. The corpses of his clan didn't seem to register in his mind. I knew what he was going to say before the words left his mouth.

"Veronica," he growled. "Where is she?"

I braced for all hell to break loose. "Not here. She was taken."

Orion's eyes blazed with a fury that might have scared me if I believed he could stand under his own power. "The beast!" he bellowed. "That fucking devil. I'll tear it apart with my bare hands." He made an attempt to leap to his feet, which nearly ended with him flat in the dirt again.

"I don't think that's a good idea right now," I said calmly, holding him up.

He glowered. "Don't forget your place, angel."

"I haven't. That's why I saved your life." Slowly, I helped Orion stand. "And it wasn't the beast who took her. It was someone else. A man."

The vampire's face tightened into a rigid mask of rage. He ground his teeth, and I wondered if he was going to attack me just to have some way to vent the emotion swirling within. I didn't fear him in his current state; far from it. He was weak for the first time since I'd met him.

But he didn't know that, or else he wouldn't hear it.

"Let me go, Logan." The demand left his lips in a snarl. "I will not be disrespected in this way." He turned on me. "Did you recognize his face? Tell me the truth!" The unasked question hung between us, silent and yet perfectly understood: *Was it Seth?*

"I didn't know him." The only concession I made was to let go of the arm Orion kept trying to wrench from my grasp. "He was human, I think." The man's face floated vaguely in my mind's eye. I'd been too focused on other things to commit his features to solid memory. What I recalled the most was dark blond hair and broad shoulders. And strength, if the ease with which he lifted Veronica was any indication.

In other words, he was likely to be yet another rival in Orion's eyes. It was exhausting just to consider the possibility, and a glance at the vampire's expression all but confirmed it. If rage could have powered him on its own, he'd have taken off into the forest long ago.

"Where did she go?" he barked. "They can't

have gone far." He lurched toward the trees. I let him go until one of his knees threatened to buckle under his weight, and then I followed reluctantly.

"I don't know," I said, keeping my voice calm and level. The urge to knock him out again rose with every outburst, but I held it in. Whatever was left of the clan would be lost completely if their leader fell. Did I care about that myself? I wasn't sure.

But deep down, I knew that Veronica might. And I still fully intended to track her down and get her back. For Orion, maybe, but at the very least, for myself.

"You don't know anything." Orion staggered. He fell forward, hard, into the churned-up earth. His fingers clenched around the soil. "Don't touch me. I'm fine."

He was obviously not fine. We both saw it. I knelt down at his side and gradually pulled him upright, slinging his arm around my shoulders.

"Let's go back to the house for now." Without giving him time to answer, I began walking toward the pathway out of the grove. It was clear that the eerie, necromantic magic that usually preserved him wasn't working at the moment. The best solution I could think of was to put him back in his tomb.

"I should be healing," he muttered. "Why isn't it working?" A note of panic stood out beneath the smoldering anger in his voice. That, I could understand; it'd probably been a few centuries since he'd felt what it was like to crawl closer and closer to death.

"You got your ass kicked," I told him. "That's why. Give it time."

Orion bristled. "We don't have time! Veronica—"

I cut him off. "If you don't shut the fuck up and let me get you back to the house, you are as good as dead. Won't be able to find her then, will you?"

He seethed into the silence but didn't say anything more.

I woke up to a foggy head, a body full of aches and pains, and a strangely familiar ceiling. The room spun when I tried to sit up, so that didn't last long. Reclining back against the pillows, I stifled a groan and tried my best not to puke.

"Are you positive?" Lian's voice, tense and questioning, filtered through the wall. I furrowed my brow and homed in on her words, wondering who she was talking to. Didn't take long for the answer to come.

"Yes, babe. I know what a wendigo looks like. I've seen them before." There was a pause. "Never here, though."

My eyes shot open immediately. A knot of

anxiety twisted itself into my stomach. Even just the sound of Trent made me inexplicably nervous. Maybe it was because I couldn't even think of him without going back to the dark, rain-slick night on the streets of Seattle where it all began.

"What is he doing here?" I whispered. Then I remembered how Lian had never stopped being in love with him, and how she'd told me she was going to call him if I didn't get my shit together. And here I was, still a passenger on the hot mess express. I really had no right to be surprised.

Not about him, at least. The wendigo, though— that was a different story. After a few solid years in the field as a professional slayer, it was one of the few supernaturals I had never seen in person. Pictures, yes. Grisly, gruesome pictures. In hindsight, I kicked myself for not thinking of it sooner. But Trent was right; I'd never heard of a wendigo showing up in Alaska.

Why now?

"Look," Trent said, "believe it or not, the wendigo isn't the important thing right now. I'll take care of it. We need to know why she was there in the first place."

"You said the vamps were dead, right? Maybe she killed them." Lian was not convinced, but she was trying her best to give me the benefit of the doubt, yet again. I chewed my lip and wondered if there was any way on earth I could have been a worse friend to her.

"No. You saw how she was dressed." Trent scoffed. "Not exactly a work uniform."

"Unless she was trying to blend in," Lian retorted. The tension between them was palpable, even from the other side of the wall.

"I doubt it," he muttered.

Uncomfortable for a whole host of reasons, I shifted in the bed. The box spring let out a piercing squeak. I froze.

Apparently Trent and Lian did the same, because then he said, "Well, why don't you go ask her?"

I let out my breath. "Shit." Trent was pissed, and they probably both had a lot of questions I didn't really want to answer. The web of deception had been spun so intricately at this point that I wasn't even sure if I had a reasonable way out right now. Maybe I just had to live with it until I found what I was looking for.

Which is what, V? The holy trinity of supernatural dick? A forbidden orgy?

The door opened. Lian crept in. She saw me

lying there with my eyes open and came quickly to the bedside. "Hey, V." Gently, she brushed a piece of hair out of my face. "How are you feeling? Welcome back to the land of the living."

I gave her a little smile and slowly sat myself up. "What are you talking about? I was totally fine." This time at least, the room didn't spin like a theme park ride.

She frowned. "You absolutely were not. Trent brought you in, and I thought you'd gotten yourself killed."

"Not quite." I chuckled wryly. "I don't think so, anyway." The memories were still a blur. I realized I had no idea how long I'd been out. "I'm surprised Trent didn't follow you in here. Figured he'd want to tear me a new one."

Lian sighed. "He does." She reached over and picked up my hand. "Veronica, I *need* you to level with me now, okay? I feel like you don't fully understand how deep in the shit you are. Trent told me about what he saw in the forest. About the vampires."

I gasped. The color drained out of my face as my memory finally kicked into high gear. It took all my willpower not to panic-shout Orion's name. The last time I saw him, he had just been tossed like a fucking rag doll. "The…the vampires?" I repeated, stunned into near-speechlessness.

Lian nodded solemnly. She squeezed my hand. "What the hell happened, V? Do you remember?"

"I…" I stared down at my lap. Inside, my mind was racing. *Is he dead now? Did Trent kill him? My most pressing question I couldn't ask.* "I guess you called him after all."

"Because you gave me no choice. I can't have you keeping secrets, V. Not when I'm the one who brought you up here. I thought we'd be doing this together, and lately I feel like you're trying to pull away." She shrugged. "It could be a slayer thing I don't understand. Trent does it too. So really, I need both of you to cut it out, please."

The guilt came back with a vengeance. "Sorry." I glanced away. "It's just…when I'm up to my neck in this bullshit, it's easy to convince myself we're all better off with me going it alone."

"Except you're not," she replied. "That's the whole point." She wrapped her other hand around mine. "And if it makes you feel better, that's not the *only* reason I asked Trent to come back."

"It's not?" Surprised, I looked up.

"My dad lost a lot of crewmen when the shifter tribe decided to bail. Business is way down." She shrugged slightly. "Trent pays me on the side to do desk work for his jobs. Research, navigation, whatever. I'm using the extra money to help with the boats."

"Fuck." I rubbed my eyes. "I forgot about that. I'm sorry, Li. This is all so fucked up."

"Yeah." She was quiet for a minute. "Which is why you have to tell me what was going on in the forest. Literally the last thing I expected was for Trent to come back with you slung over his shoulder like that. Scared me half to death."

I should have come clean right then, as she sat on the side of the bed in the guest room with me. That was my chance to lay everything on the table and own up to all the trouble I'd gotten in. Trent wasn't even there, though I had no doubt he could hear me if he wanted to, just like I was able to hear him. It was just me and her, like old times.

But for some reason, I couldn't force myself to open up. Not even after she asked me to as directly as she knew how. It made me feel like shit, and yet, I couldn't change the words that came out of my mouth.

"I don't recall anything beyond the wendigo crashing the party." That much was the truth. It also didn't answer her question.

"But what *happened*, Veronica? What were you doing there?" Her face had grown deadly serious. "You can't tell me there wasn't a real good reason and expect me to believe it."

"I was gathering intel." I spoke as casually as possible, as if I hadn't been hauled to safety by my best friend's boyfriend like a magical sack of potatoes. "Things got out of hand."

"Okay, but how did you get in? Who invited you?" The pressure was on. I felt her maneuvering me into a corner so that she could press me for as much information as I would give up. I looked at her hands, still holding on to mine, and wondered if Trent had coached her before she walked in.

"Listen, I get that you don't want me leaving you out of the loop, and I'm sorry it's kind of been that way lately. But I can't just tell you everything I know. Some of this stuff could put a target on your back, Li. Ask Trent if you need to hear it from him. He understands even better than I do."

She examined me searchingly. "I don't blame you, V. And I think some of what you're saying is the truth. But I also kind of think you're full of shit right now, and I don't get why." She paused. "This is why Trent came to Anchorage."

"I'm glad he did," I answered. "Honestly. I have zero practical experience with wendigos."

She was trying so hard not to roll her eyes into next week. "All right, all right, fine. Do you want to talk to him about it?"

"Only if you make him promise not to bite my head off." I wanted the knowledge Trent had, but not the lectures or suspicion that were sure to come with it. He wasn't wrong, per se, but he didn't need to know that.

"He won't," she said. "I made him swear he wouldn't play hardball—at least not right away."

I smirked. "I appreciate the effort."

Lian got up and went to the door, opened it, and stuck her head out. She said his name, and a moment later, Trent stepped into the bedroom. He and I stared at each other for a couple minutes that might as well have been days.

"Hey, Veronica." When he finally spoke, his tone was more subdued than I expected. "How are you feeling?"

"Uh…I'm okay." I shot Lian a glance that was half confused, half impressed. Trent had always been a little wild, a little unpredictable. Maybe she'd managed to tame him somehow. Or maybe life had done the heavy lifting for her in that regard. "Thanks for getting me out of there."

"Don't mention it." He sat down in a chair across from the foot of the bed. His eyes were exactly the shade of clear sea-green I remembered, but they were haunted now by ghosts of the past. The same ghosts who haunted me.

The quiet returned and soon became crushing. I was the one who broke first. "So…" A lame start, but one of us had to say something, or else the air would just keep slowly draining from the room.

Trent half smiled. "Been a long time, hasn't it?" he said.

CHAPTER 16

ORION

I had no thoughts in my head that didn't concern Veronica. Where perhaps there ought to have been gratitude toward Logan for pulling me back from the edge of oblivion, I was filled with hatred for the one who had swooped in and stolen her away.

He was an outsider. He had to be. Not a soul in Anchorage, living or dead, would have shown me such blatant disrespect. And when I found this mysterious man, I'd make sure that taking Veronica was the last mistake he'd ever make.

"You didn't see his face?" I demanded yet again. Even I had long ago lost track of how many times that question had leapt off my tongue, but I couldn't let it go. My very sanity depended on unlocking the secret of the man's identity so that I could recover Veronica—and exact vengeance. "Think!"

Logan shook his head. "I saw very little," he said flatly. "As I've told you, my concerns were focused elsewhere at the time." At any other time, it would have been abundantly clear that his patience was being stretched thin. But I didn't care. I wasn't able to. Until Veronica was found, nothing else in the entire universe mattered as much as her whereabouts.

"How could he touch her?" Unable to stay still, I stormed around the first floor of the house, where Logan had forced me to stay. Anything that wasn't nailed down had been thrown or upended—broken objects littered the floor. The chairs in the dining room lay in a heap, and I snatched one of the legs as I went by, striking it against my palm. "Does he have any idea what he's done?"

"I doubt it very much." Logan's tone remained icy, detached. He stared at me with a bored expression, though his eyes tracked my movement closely. "But we both know Anchorage is full of people who can handle themselves in…unique situations."

I whipped around to glower at him. "What are

you saying? That this was planned? That I've been tricked?" The very notion of a plot coming to fruition without my knowledge stoked the fire of my anger to a fever pitch. The humiliation of being outfoxed—by a human, no less—was a handful of salt in a fresh, raw wound.

The fallen angel sighed. He displayed no fear, only mild annoyance. "He could have had help." He paused. "Maybe from her."

The blow of his words left me stunned for a moment. I understood as well as anyone that Veronica and I had no formal contract, no relationship beyond the mutual attraction that kept drawing us together. Indeed, she'd made her stance clear just recently, hadn't she? We were free agents, as far as she was concerned, two bodies often passing in rapid orbit.

But my desire for her led me to make certain assumptions. Most prominently that she was mine, and it was simply a matter of time before I could make our bond official. Now, those plans had been tossed into jeopardy by this infernal interloper.

"I have to turn her," I muttered. The thought was so automatic and unconscious that I didn't realize it had escaped my lips until I noticed Logan looking at me. Immediately, I was on the defensive. "Not a fucking word. I can't risk losing her."

He was silent, for a while. Just long enough to make me think perhaps he hadn't heard me, or hadn't heard correctly.

Then he said, "You won't be able to do that. Not in the way you think."

It was the kind of insubordination I might have expected from Seth, but never Logan. The conviction in his voice, so cold and calm, was deeply unnerving. He made no move to explain further, and I found myself not wanting to ask. Maybe this was just another personal oddity, of which he had many.

That resolve lasted less than a minute. "What do you mean?" I snapped. I was in no mood for his typically enigmatic phrases. My body had barely begun to heal from the injuries I'd sustained in the encounter at the grove; I was impatient and on edge. Logan had picked the worst time to voice dissent I didn't want to hear anyway.

Still, something told me to bite my tongue, which I did with great effort. He took his sweet time formulating an answer.

At long last, he said, "It won't work."

And that terse, three-word response was the

breaking point for me. My temper, already fraught with cracks like a flawed pane of glass, shattered into a thousand vicious shards. I wheeled and leapt at him, fangs suddenly bared.

"I have had *enough* of this bullshit!" I expected to land on top of him, seize him by the shirt. Instead, he outmaneuvered my dull reflexes, and I struck the chair where he'd been sitting as it toppled over. The edge of the seat slammed into my stomach.

From somewhere above me, Logan said, "With all due respect, you're not in any position to say so." He stepped up alongside me and hauled me to my feet. "Look, Orion. If you really want to fight about this, let's fight. But I'm just trying to warn you that what you want for Veronica isn't possible."

I didn't give him a proper answer; I just punched him in the face. It was not a strong punch, and Logan seemed to shrug it off immediately. The burst of exertion caused my surroundings to sway and shimmer. I felt my eyes threatening to roll back in my head. Why wasn't my fucking body cooperating? I hadn't lived for centuries to lose a skirmish against one of my own henchmen.

"Fuck off," I told him unconvincingly. "It was a

mistake to think I needed either of you. Wherever Seth is, I hope you end up there too."

I might as well have been insulting a brick wall. Logan pulled back and returned the hit I doled out —except his was undiluted by weakness. My head rocked backward. I heard something crack. A tooth, perhaps, or maybe my neck. The as-yet-unheeded whisper of common sense in the back of my mind told me I was being uncharacteristically foolish, that he could kill me while the scales were so unbalanced.

Part of me wished he would. For the first time in ages, I was useless, incapacitated by unforeseen limits. And my rage was beginning to give way to a frightening level of despair. How had I come to rely on Veronica so heavily? Long ago, I swore it would never happen again, and yet here I was, locked in a grapple with a fallen angel, half on the floor of the house we shared.

Seen from the outside, the image must have been surreal. Logan had his hand on my throat, his grip solid as steel. His wings had come out when I sprang, and now they cast me in menacing shadow. His eyes, inches from my face, were placid, glacial.

"Take a moment to look around and see where

you are," he said quietly. "And act accordingly." His thumb and index finger braced against the corners of my jaw. The heel of his hand pressed gently but firmly into my Adam's apple. It was no more than a warning. But I understood.

"I ought to kill you when this is over," I muttered. "I'd be doing both of us a favor."

"Yes," Logan agreed. "You probably would." He planted his knee down on my chest and let go of my face. "You're being naïve about Veronica, despite the years you've spent among mortals. She's more complex than you give her credit for."

"And you know this, how?" The storm of fury died down as quickly as it arrived. More disgruntled by the ease of my defeat than anything, I pulled the chair out from underneath my back and lay flat on the floor. Logan did not move. I supposed I couldn't blame him. Were I at full strength, he'd be a pile of sinew and bloody feathers.

"Her spirit is unique." He stared off into space as he talked about her. "Don't you feel it?"

"Of course I do." I tried not to sulk. It stung to know I wasn't the only one who thought Veronica special.

Logan nodded. "That's why you're obsessed."

I didn't bother denying it. "Whatever game we're playing, I'm going to win it. Veronica will join the clan." Formerly, my word was law, among clan members and other associates alike.

This time, Logan looked at me. "What clan?" he asked wryly.

I glared. "You've already won. For now."

He was quiet. After a few moments, he got up and backed away, keeping his gaze pinned on me. "Don't do anything stupid, Orion. We've just proven you're in no shape to pursue her, and contrary to popular belief, my goodwill isn't infinite."

"Yeah, yeah." I lay on my back and let my eyes drift closed. Rest was the last thing I wanted, but my battered body begged to differ. Pain had become almost a foreign sensation, but I savored it the same as pleasure. If only its presence didn't indicate that the magic I relied on for so long had nearly failed.

"Logan."

"Yes." His tone implied heavily that he wished I hadn't spoken. The single syllable was frosted with irritation.

"Thank you for bringing me back. You didn't have to."

He hesitated. "Yes, I did. You're lucky for it. And you are welcome."

With that, the choppy waters between us seemed to settle. Eventually, I sensed his eye drawn away, lured by boredom or perhaps by some ethereal thing I couldn't see. He hadn't left his post, but the bulk of his attention had wandered. I took a deep breath, opened my mind's eye, and began the search for Veronica.

Logan may have won the physical fight, but there was nothing across any plane that could keep her away from me. Veronica was mine, and she'd been stolen without honor.

I refused to let her go.

Things had very nearly gotten out of hand. I went back over every detail of our little skirmish in my mind as Orion lay where he'd fallen on the hardwood, doing a remarkable imitation of a corpse. He could not, however, mask his now stable aura, the shroud of spirit and energy that flowed around him. Although he was weak, he had clawed his way back from danger. Even if he didn't feel it yet.

But it was still a fine balance to maintain. The fight, small as it was, had nearly wiped his reserves clean out. I would've been lying if I said I didn't think about ending things for good in the seconds he spent under my thumb. So simple to crush his windpipe, or cave in his chest with the point of my knee. What would he have done?

Nothing. He was helpless. I wondered how that felt to such an aged and powerful being, to be reduced to an animated shell of skin and bones. Did it scare him to be reminded of what it was like to be human; to be mortal?

I glanced at the chair he'd pushed away. Any of its four legs could easily be fashioned into an impromptu stake. He must have known how vulnerable he was, lying supine with his eyes closed, outwardly at rest. I imagined piercing his cold, dead heart, impaling him through into the floor.

A smooth, swift motion. Simple. Effortless, even.

Why not?

I looked around, startled. The thought had not come from inside my own head, but from somewhere beyond. The words had not been spoken as much as felt, projected into my consciousness. I called up my spirit sense, probing the glimmering veil between this realm and the next for their source.

Look at the bastard. He's probably half dead as is. You'd be doing him a favor.

"Ah," I murmured under my breath. Now I recognized him. "Where are you?" As I spoke, I kept one eye on Orion, just in case he decided to try and make a move.

I don't know. In a room with a bunch of mirrors. Think I finally figured out how to use 'em. There was a pause. *Well, sort of.*

"Is it cold there?" I asked. Talking out loud was unnecessary, but it helped to anchor me, so that I didn't just drift off in automatic pursuit of Seth's essence. Personally, I yearned to be somewhere, anywhere other than in the house with Orion in his current state. My dutiful obligation to him had faded.

Yeah, it's fuckin' cold here. You goddamned angels and your frigid hellscapes. I don't know how you live with this shit.

"I take it you're not enjoying yourself, then." I smirked. Couldn't help it. I had no visual on him, but even his voice sounded haggard, rougher than usual. A humbling experience for a prince of Hell —if he could be humbled in the first place.

I've been better, he grumbled. Then he said, *There's gotta be a way to cross back over from here. I need you to help me do it.*

"Oh, do you?" Just what I needed: another

pushy, arrogant prick with a bad temper. But there was no denying that Orion had gotten himself into dire straits. I could admit that help of some kind would be useful. "What's in it for me?"

I'll help you find the slayer.

I'd expected him to bargain, or to have some kind of snarky retort at the ready. "You know she's gone?"

Saw it happen. The mirrors show me everything. I got a pretty good look at the guy who snatched her up.

I chuckled grimly. "Don't tell that to the leader." Neither of us needed to be told that Orion would lose his shit if he thought he had a chance to identify the man he considered a thief of his prize possession.

I don't plan on it. If he wants her, he'll have to find her himself. He paused. *Tell me how to get the fuck out of here, angel boy. Before I fucking freeze to death.*

"Give me a second to think about it." I leaned back in my seat, mulling over what I'd just learned. The long and short of it seemed to be that Seth was trapped in some layer of the Underworld— farther down, judging by the temperature. How he got there, I didn't know.

But I had spent considerable time in those frigid circles long ago, just after the fall that made me an angel, and I knew there had to be some way out, even for a person like Seth. No doubt he would immediately become a pain in the ass again once he'd returned to the mortal realm. Still, I wanted Veronica back. Preferably with as little involvement from Orion as possible.

"He might kill you if he thinks you're becoming competition," I warned.

The impression of a laugh echoed through the veil. *Who, the vamp? Let him try.*

That was when the connection between us began to waver. As he started to fade back into the ether, I reached out on instinct to try and grab him. At the same time, my anchor in the mortal realm slipped a little. For a moment or two, my concentration slipped, and I straddled the border between realms. The frigid rock walls of the Underworld loomed suddenly in front of me, and then they were gone.

"Shit," I whispered.

What was that? Don't tell me you fell through.

"No." Without opening my eyes, I ran a hand through my hair. "No, I'm fine. This might be a good sign for you, actually."

Yeah? It'd be the first in a while. Lay it on me.

I frowned. A thought had just occurred to me.

If the paths were open enough to allow Seth to slip through, he likely wasn't the only one who would be trying. Maybe the monster running rampant in the forest wouldn't be the only one for very long.

"Are you alone?" I asked.

Was starting to think you forgot about me. Yeah, I'm alone...mostly.

I furrowed my brow. "What does that mean? Who else is there?"

No one special. Just some gremlins and angry spirits who want me off their turf. The usual.

"You'll have to take care of them," I told him. "We can't risk you being watched or followed."

At first, I thought he might object. Then I remembered who I was talking to. *No problem. Give me a minute. Two minutes, if they're lucky.* The aura of his presence melted away, and I opened my eyes. The passage of time had been blurred by intense concentration; stepping back into the physical realm came with an adjustment.

Suddenly, everything stopped completely, as if the great internal clock of the universe had just ceased its ticking. The spot where Orion had lain was empty. And there was no sign of him to be found.

I stood up so fast that the chair toppled over.

"Damn it." Glancing toward the house's entryway, I saw that he had left the door hanging open, swinging slightly on its hinges. I had one foot on the porch by the time Seth came back to his side of the veil.

What the fuck are you doing now?

"Orion left." I grimaced. "While we were talking."

So what? Maybe he'll die out there. I saw what happened to him and his whole clan.

Of course he still didn't think of us as a team after he got shoved into that place, or probably much of anything outside himself. After taking in a sweeping panoramic view of my surroundings to no avail, I shook my head, gave up, and went back inside. Orion was hardly in the best shape he'd ever been, but if he felt well enough to bail out on his own, I reasoned that my priority had to be finding Veronica. Because I didn't really want him to get to her first.

"All right, listen. I'm assuming you can see things through those mirrors."

Yeah. You, him, the slayer girl, and the thing that kicked their asses.

"Her name is Veronica," I said. "And those are shitty choices, but they'll have to do." That particular arrangement of mirrors meant we only had one realistically viable option. Which, at the very least, streamlined the decision-making process.

I didn't know you cared. Seth sounded genuinely surprised, and perhaps even impressed. I could practically picture him standing on the frozen rock, eyebrow arched, arms crossed.

I shrugged. "Don't we all?"

Yeah. I guess we fuckin' do.

Unwilling to dwell on the subject, I pushed forward. "Anyway, pay attention. Each of the mirrors has a link to the person whose perspective they show, which means they're all linked to this realm. The realm you want to be in."

Uh huh. I think I get where this is going.

"Right now, those connections are stable and secure. But if you were to break one of those mirrors…" I trailed off, inviting him to fill in the blank.

You saying I might be able to bust my way through a broken link?

"Yes." I exhaled a sigh of relief. "The only thing is, breaking that connection won't be good for whoever you choose."

That right? He was quiet for a few seconds too long, clearly considering more options than I had.

Give me one good reason I shouldn't step on Orion's neck on my way in.

I rolled my eyes. Was it always going to be such a dick-measuring contest with these guys? "Maybe you won't consider this a good reason, but I don't know what would happen to you if he died before you got all the way through. And honestly, I'm not sure he'd make it."

If you're trying to make me feel sorry for him, it's not gonna work.

"I could not care less how you feel about him," I admitted. "Or about him in general, frankly. But Veronica might."

Fuck. I got a very strong sense of Seth face-palming, holding his head in his hands. *Fine. I'll take the monster.*

Another wave of relief surged through me, for an entirely different reason. "Good. Warn me when—"

Predictably, there was no warning at all. The shockwave created by the shattering mirror reverberated across dimensions, briefly graying out the colors in my vision and making the world warp inward. The fabric of the veil, already stretched thin in many places, tore open, letting in a burst of spirit energy that threatened to destabilize the makeshift doorway I'd been straddling between the realms. A sharp pain rocketed through my temples. I gritted my teeth.

But the plan appeared to work. Once the sparks of light and pain stopped dancing behind my eyelids, I stretched out a curious feeler for Seth on the correct side of the veil. I found him exactly where I'd predicted he would land—deep in the forest that housed Orion's secret grove. His energy burned strong, like a flare on a moonless night. He was definitely in the right realm now.

The real question was, what had happened to the monster whose body he'd used as a vessel? Was it dead? And if not, was it angry?

As soon as I finished regathering my wits, I headed out the open door, closing it behind me. The bleak Alaskan landscape rolled out in all directions. I ran forward, unfurling my wings, catching the edge of the brisk, sharp wind. Beneath me, the land fell rapidly away, and I banked around toward the dark tide of woods blanketing the west.

Did I want to go anywhere near the vampire grove? Absolutely not. But I knew I had no choice. No point in helping Seth cross over if I was just going to leave him to die. Most likely, he thought he could handle himself without a problem. Every time I thought about turning back, though, the sight of Orion's crumpled body flashed through my mind, followed closely by the single glimpse I'd gotten of Veronica hanging limply over a stranger's shoulder.

We needed her back—if only because it was starting to seem like we might have finally stumbled in over our heads.

CHAPTER 18

VERONICA

I had never felt so uncomfortable in the Zhou family home. It was so weird and wrong to be tense under their roof, considering how much time I'd spent basically living as a second daughter when I would visit as kids. But as I sat awkwardly in the bed, hands clasped in my lap, avoiding Trent's gaze, I just wanted to disappear. I should have known that Lian called her ex to get involved in my shit. Not that I can complain considering how badly crap went down at Orion's vampire meeting, but still. The moment I was dreading had finally arrived.

"Yeah." My voice came out raspy. I cleared my throat. If I could've, I would have paid Trent any amount of money to leave the room and never come back—at least not for the rest of the day. It was nothing against him as a person, really. He'd been my best friend's lover and obsession for years and years, and when they were on, he treated her like a queen. I should've loved him.

But he was too real, sitting less than ten feet away from me. I preferred him when he was traveling, because then it was easier to pretend all of the memories in which he featured prominently never happened, that they were masochistic fantasies in my head. Seeing Trent in any capacity meant confronting the past. Even if he didn't bring it up. He'd been close friends with my ex, Dylan, and had come up to Seattle many times to fight with us, to catch up.

Both of us were great at stewing in heavy silence. It drove Lian insane.

"Listen," he said softly. "I know this is weird. It's weird for me too, I promise." His eyes wandered around the room. I wondered what he was thinking. "I guess it doesn't help that we haven't spoken much since Dylan died."

I winced. As far as I was concerned, things would've been perfectly fine had he never once mentioned that particular elephant in the room. In fact, I'd gone so far as to assume the subject would remain unaddressed. I wasn't emotionally prepared to remember my ex-boyfriend's death, let alone examine it in granular detail.

"Trent…" I had no idea what the hell I was going to say—just that I had to say something, anything, to get him to veer off from where we were headed. "Hey, thanks for saving me back there. You didn't have to." The transition, if you could call it that, was about as smooth and graceful as a burning car rolling down an embankment. I might as well have worn a neon sign that read, DO NOT TALK TO ME ABOUT THIS.

He glanced at me, startled. "What?" Obviously, I had interrupted some invisible train of thought. A planned confrontation, maybe? The irrational paranoia invading my brain insisted that he was about to dredge up some serious mud, lay everything out on the line. We were suddenly a train speeding toward a moment of emotional catharsis. For him, of course. Not me.

I sucked in a breath, trying to disguise the evidence of my spiking anxiety. "You didn't have to save my life," I told him. "God knows you don't owe me anything." Despite my sincerest efforts, I thought of Dylan as I spoke, how he'd died in the rain-soaked street in Seattle so many years ago while I watched the life drain from his eyes, helpless. How Trent had arrived moments after to see me crying over Dylan's death as I lost sight of the vampires who dragged him away from me. Sharpness cut into my heart, slicing me over and over like Dylan's death just happened.

The air caught in my throat. I swallowed hard. Without even trying, I'd gone plummeting back to the place I'd been trying to escape since the night it happened.

Trent frowned. "What the hell are you talking about, Veronica?" The way he spoke was brusque, but with an undertone of empathy.

"You know." I cleared my throat again, struggled to push down the lump that kept trying to form. "You know exactly what I mean."

He didn't answer right away. I heard him sigh and run his fingers through his dark blond hair. From the outside, we must have looked like a scene from some daytime drama. Two old friends reuniting at last, a hatchet unburied between them. Except with us, the hatchet was a corpse belonging to someone we'd both loved in vastly different ways.

"It's not your fault," Trent said at last. "None of

it. Okay? There was nothing you could've done to change anything that happened."

I laughed painfully, my lips twisting into a stark caricature of a smile. "I wish I could get myself to believe that." In my lap, my restless hands trembled. "I was right there, Trent. Right there. So close, and yet…" My voice trailed off. What else was there to say? Certainly nothing I hadn't said a million times before.

"I don't know how to help you," Trent admitted. "But all that stuff with Dylan—it's not on you, V. Who you are now isn't who you were back then. It's all in the past." He looked as if he was about to say something else, then changed his mind and stayed quiet.

"Yeah." I nodded robotically. "You're right. I just…have to keep telling myself."

"Every day," Trent agreed solemnly. "I get it." He stared out the window. "But that's not why we're here right now." The energy in the room shifted. A shiver ran down my spine. My hands squeezed each other tightly. I steeled myself.

"What do you want to know?" A loaded question. A dangerous question. If I had struggled omitting the truth from my conversation with Lian, Trent's slayer senses made lying all but impossible. Not only would he see right through me, he'd call me out on it too. Trying to talk my way to safety would be a futile exercise.

I was standing at the edge of a minefield, about to take the first step.

"The grove." He pulled exactly zero punches right out of the gate. "How did you get in?" Lian had asked the same thing, but Trent's tone carried much more weight. He had turned his full attention on me. I sensed the walls closing in.

"He invited me." Maintaining eye contact was excruciating, but necessary. I refused to seem vulnerable or afraid, even though there was a little bit of both simmering in my emotions. "And I'm trying my best to get inside his head, so of course I said yes."

"Who's 'he'?" Trent asked. "The clanmaster?"

I nodded casually. "Orion. No surname that I know of." *That's it, V. You're a colleague, not a criminal. Don't give him any reason to suspect you.*

"Yeah. They usually lose the family names after a couple generations, if they don't just ditch them entirely." He paused. "Did you find anything out?"

"Nah." I shook my head. "Unfortunately, the party was crashed before we got to the good stuff. And, well…" I shrugged. "Now most of them are gone, so whatever his plans were, they have a giant wrench thrown right in the middle."

"And he didn't tell you about those plans prior to the meeting?" Trent kept things cordial, but I could feel his interest ratcheting up. Here was where he expected to catch me in a lie, possibly the first of many. And to his credit, I was tempted.

"Well, I think there were more in the works," I said. "But he did say he wanted to go down to Seattle and issue a reverse challenge on their clan. Retaliation for them sticking their noses in Anchorage business, I guess. I assumed he'd be discussing the logistics of a clan-to-clan challenge at the meeting."

"But he never got that far," Trent finished.

"Right. Because a certain homicidal uninvited guest decided to show up last minute."

"Hm." Trent studied the floor, deep in thought. "You know, he's lucky he hasn't seen a wendigo up to this point. I'd think they'd be way into all the blood-drinking these guys are doing." He furrowed his brow. "Although is it technically cannibalism?"

I saw an opportunity to divert the uncomfortably hot spotlight and jumped at it. "Tell me about the wendigo. I really wish I'd gotten a better look." I had no idea we were dealing with a wendigo and now this started to explain the killings in town.

"No, you don't." Trent smirked grimly. "Those things are utter nightmares. I knew a guy who came face to face with one and was never the same. The fact that there's even one in the area is pretty bad news."

"You're telling me. It's been racking up a body count since before I got here."

"Not good," Trent murmured. "The more it kills, the stronger it'll be. No wonder it tore the vamps apart." He stood up abruptly. "Eventually it'll be unkillable. We've got to get to it first.' He turned to me. "And by 'we,' I mean me. You shouldn't go anywhere for now."

"I'm fine," I protested, without really knowing if I was or not. "This is just as much my problem as it is yours, Trent. I'm not going to be shoved off the case."

"No one's shoving you off," he replied. "Just take it easy, for Lian's sake. She's—"

His sentence was cut short by the kind of scream that curdles human blood. We froze, and then both of us bolted from the bedroom. I was out of the bed so fast, I barely felt my feet touch the hardwood floor. The steps flew by at dangerous, breakneck speeds. There was only one other person in the house who could be screaming like that; the very person Trent and I wanted to protect the most.

Lian stood in the front entryway, barefoot, her hands clamped tightly over her mouth. The door to the house hung ajar, but I couldn't see what might be in the doorway. As we approached, Lian turned toward Trent and let him get in front of her. His eyes flicked forward, and then immediately to my face.

"What is it?" I asked. "Let me see."

Trent said nothing as I came within view of the porch. At first, my brain had a hard time making sense of what it was seeing. I thought I was looking at a large bundle of black rags, or an old blanket. A second later, however, the splayed limbs and glimpses of pale skin clicked into place.

And to my shock and horror, I recognized the face lying against the cold concrete.

"Stay back," Trent warned. "Looks like a vamp. He could be dead, but you know how hard it is to tell with these bastards." He stepped forward. "I'll take care of him in a second."

Instant panic flashed through my body. I had to force myself not to lunge at Trent to try and hold him back. Normally, Orion could've given even the most seasoned slayer a run for their money. But he looked like absolute shit out there. He didn't stand a chance.

"Trent, wait!" My exclamation was met by stunned silence. Trent and Lian both stared at me. An inscrutable expression crept into his gaze.

"For what?" He spoke slowly. "You want it to be a fair fight?"

"No." I put my hand on his arm. "Just wait, okay? Trust me."

It was a tall order, but he complied, albeit reluctantly. He moved back, and I bent down to get a closer look at Orion. The vamp was out cold, eyes half rolled back in his head, skin waxy and grayish. Had he come straight from the skirmish with the wendigo?

Not that it really mattered. I had way bigger problems than the wendigo now, including the fact that Orion had apparently turned up on Lian's porch to flirt with death. My mind raced as I attempted to figure out a solution. But the truth was, I had no idea what the hell to do. And my friends weren't going to wait forever.

CHAPTER 19

SETH

The first thing I noticed upon my triumphant return to the mortal realm was the blessed rise in temperature. No longer did the bone-gnawing cold make every organ in my body ache, including my skin. I would've stood there for a while in the dank little cave where I'd landed, just enjoying the great thaw—except that something else snagged my attention as soon as I opened my eyes.

The beast whose eyes I had been borrowing lay at my feet, stunned, injured, or both. Its skeletal ribcage heaved, and I could see the glistening walls of its partially exposed heart contracting in a frenzied bid to keep it on this side of the veil. Despite its sorry state, or perhaps because of it, the thing was not happy to see me. It reared back its head and let out a plaintive, hollow cry.

"Really?" I stepped over one long, splayed out arm, dodging a weak attempt to snatch my leg. I had expected the possibility of a fight once I'd made it back to mortal soil, but this monstrosity was in such bad shape I couldn't bring myself to raise a hand against it. The light burning deep within its empty eye sockets flickered unsteadily.

Once more, it tried to grab me, and again I sidestepped. This time, I saw something caught on its long, vicious claws—a scrap of dark fabric. With one swoop of my hand, I grabbed the swatch and held it up. There was no mistaking Orion's distinctive, pompous aura. The cloth reeked of it.

"Should've fucking known," I muttered. To the wretched beast, I said, "I can't believe you let *him* do this to you, of all people."

It thrashed angrily by way of a response. Stepping away from the collapsed heap of bones and sinew, I began to search for further evidence of the vampire's trail. He wasn't the one I was interested in, of course. But I knew enough to surmise that if he was out in the forest tangling with eyeless skull-beasts after getting his ass kicked once already, it was probably because of the slayer.

Which meant finding him would invariably bring me that much closer to finding her.

Ten yards from the downed creature, I found another scrap of fabric among the debris littering the forest floor. Aside from some dirt, it was clean and bloodless, saturated with his energy. I turned it over in my hands, running my thumb across the material. Traces of the girl were in there too.

"You better hope I don't find you alive," I remarked to no one. "Or else you're never gonna live this down."

From behind, the injured beast called out again. I looked over my shoulder to see it struggling to stand, all fucked up and bent out of shape. One foot hung limply by the thinnest thread of tissue. Its baleful glare locked on to me, and I tensed without thinking. The charge that came next was slow and shambling, a mistake on the aggressor's part. Its warbling, unearthly cry seemed like a dying monster's last stand.

I felt kind of bad as I watched it come toward me. The spirit of its rage was still there, which I could appreciate, but the body was falling apart. Whatever challenge once existed had been beaten out by other opponents, leaving me with a broken-down shell of a creature hardly worth the effort of putting it down.

As its shadow loomed over me, I reached up and grabbed on to one of its curved ribs. The combination of my strength and its momentum tore the bone loose from its socket. The snapping of bone and tendon rang like a visceral gunshot through the trees.

The beast shrieked. There was something arrestingly human about the way it wailed, with notes of bereavement and rage in addition to injury. I jumped aside, still holding the broken rib. The creature had reared all the way back on its hind legs. Long fingers grasped urgently at the hole the rib had left.

"Sorry." I held up the bone. "You want it back? Come get it." Its surface was splashed with cried blood that flaked off onto my skin. I waved it a little, fully expecting its owner to make some attempt to reclaim it.

But the monster just looked between me and the jagged hole in the side of its chest. Then it turned and galloped unsteadily off into the dwindling space between the trees, in the opposite direction as his trail suggested Orion had gone.

Normally, I might have pursued it until it either dropped or turned to finish the fight.

Now I had other things on my mind—one other thing, specifically. And I needed to find that bastard vamp before he got to her first.

Orion's lack of blood had never really bothered me until the moment I was trying to track him through dense forest. I tossed the rib away, keeping one ear open in case its owner decided to loop around for a second pass. No more scraps of his clothes turned up, but I could see patches of loose, recently disturbed debris on the forest floor. His energy stood out like a signal flare in these places.

In one spot, it appeared that he had lain or fallen prone for some time. I could see the outline of his body in the groundcover. That told me if I was lucky, I'd be happening upon a corpse not too far away.

I smiled a little. What poetic justice it would've been for that prick to die such an ignominious death. Alone in the woods, his clan in ruins, struck down by a creature he failed to control in the same way he manipulated so many others. I couldn't have written a more perfect ending myself.

But alas, it was not to be. I followed the spotty

trail of Orion's energy through wilderness that did not thin until the moment I stepped out on the shoulder of a paved road. The transition between wild woods and evidence of civilization was jarring, but it took no time at all to regain my bearings. More concerning was the fact that the remains of Orion's energy trail were gradually growing fainter.

Could it be that he really was dying? I didn't let my hopes get *too* high. The trail, though diluted, stayed fairly consistent. Once out of the trees, he had made his way along the road. I saw where he'd stopped to rest, where he'd stubbornly lurched forward to carry on. Even after houses began to appear at the end of winding personal lanes, Orion kept going.

No doubt he was looking for the slayer. But what the hell was she doing here, of all places? I'd grown used to seeing and hearing of her in the shadows of Anchorage, the seedy places where her prey preferred to congregate. The homes at the ends of these lanes were symbols of wealth and prestige, arrogance and greed. The lethal spirit of Alaska's frontiers neutered by piles of money.

"I thought she was here to clean up the streets,"

I muttered. It appeared that the slayer might have a benefactor footing the bill for her noble quest.

It amused me to imagine what that person might think to see Orion on their doorstep, likely half-dead and demanding an audience with their hired help. Still moving cautiously, I picked up the pace. That was one show I didn't want to miss.

And as it turned out, I was just about on time. Approaching the mouth of the next private little drive, I heard a blistering scream. Instinct told me this was the place, and so I broke into a flat run, heading toward the as-yet invisible house. Gravel flew from under my feet, scattering off to either side. I started to notice similar impressions already pressed into the stones—Orion's footprints.

They were uneven, and I noted a few spots where it looked like he had fallen. When the house came into view, there was gravel tracked up the steps to the wraparound porch, leading straight to his body collapsed in front of the open door. There was a familiar man standing in the doorway, staring down at the unwelcome arrival.

"Trent, wait!" It was her voice that struck the chord with me, though. I stopped dead, half in the open, suddenly hungry for a glimpse of her. She didn't make me wait. But I bristled at the sight of her touching his arm, looking up into his eyes, speaking soft words to him.

Who the fuck is *this guy?* Moments after having the thought, it dawned on me how much I was acting like Orion. Couldn't exactly upbraid the guy for dragging his sorry ass to her door when I was standing thirty feet behind him for the same fucking reason.

The blond stranger who had come and collected V now stood near her and told V nothing in response. So she definitely knew him.

He ceded to her authority, and she knelt down beside Orion's body. Sensing an opportunity to get the hell out of there, I went to make my retreat, but I wasn't fast enough. My movement must have triggered her senses, because her head snapped up instantly, eyes homing in with laser precision on me.

"Fuck," I whispered. With nothing to lose, I bailed as fast as I could.

"Hey!" She had definitely seen me. I felt as much as I heard her tearing down off the porch after me, her heart racing in her chest. And whether it was subconscious or not, I slowed down just enough to let her catch up without too much of an effort. "Stop!" she shouted.

I turned around. The look on her face made me think she might keel over right there, out as cold as Orion.

"Hey," I said casually. "What do you want? I'd rather not stick around, if you don't mind."

She took a deep breath. "Seth?"

"Congratulations on remembering my name," I retorted. "Can I go before your friend comes and carves me up like a fucking roast?"

My words had little impact. "You're back," she said.

"Yeah, and I'm trying to leave again." To emphasize my point, I took an exaggerated step away from her. "Call me when you sort out whatever crazy shit is going on back there."

Panic struck her eyes for a split second, as if she'd just remembered the whole scene. "No, wait. Please wait." She let out her breath. "I need your help."

I laughed. "With him? Hell no. You think I don't know he hasn't spent a second looking for me? He's fine on his own, or at least he thinks he is."

"And he's clearly wrong about that." Her answer was quick and sharp. "Seth, please. I don't know what to do, and if I do nothing at all, he'll die. He looks like shit."

"Don't have to tell me twice." The last thing I wanted to do was expend a single drop of effort to aid Orion in any way. And yet, I could already feel my resolve weakening. She was right there, mere feet away from me, and I didn't have it in me to say no.

Which made no sense. There was nothing special about this fledgling slayer aside from her hair—except that there was, and I felt it whenever I had contact with her. As much as I worked to deny it, a connection was forming between us—which was why I was there in the first place.

"Just this once," she said quietly. "I'll make it up to you."

I wasn't typically one to do favors on credit alone. But it was becoming increasingly apparent that this girl was the exception to the rule. I glowered every step of the way up to the house, including while I slung Orion over my shoulder and started to haul him back the way I'd come. He was maddeningly heavy, the epitome of dead weight.

Veronica waited for me at the lower part of the gravel drive, just out of sight of the house. "Thank you," she said, and before I had the chance to respond, she leaned up and kissed me. "I won't forget this. Promise you'll make sure he's actually on the mend."

I glared at her, then softened. "Yeah, yeah. You better remember this for the rest of your life, girl."

"My name's Veronica," she answered. She was already retracing her path up the lane. "Maybe you should use it once in a while."

"God damn it," I muttered. Casting a sidelong glance at the vamp weighing me down, I frowned once more. "This is all your fucking fault, you dick."

I hadn't made the promise that I wouldn't let him die. Not outright. But I already knew I'd keep it, because she had asked me to.

Flying low to the treetops meant flirting with potential disaster, but the woods were so dense I couldn't see a thing from too far up. The undersides of my wings skimmed along tree branches, loose feathers cascading down in my wake. I peered down through the thick canopy, searching for signs of Orion or the monster coming to finish him off.

The flight gave me plenty of time to consider what I might do if I found one or the other. Would I step in and save Orion for the second time in the past day? Would I stand back and hope another beating could finally pound some sense into him? Would I let him be torn apart and then tell Veronica there was nothing to be done?

Just imagining the latter scenario made me cringe a little. I might have felt a staggering level of apathy toward Orion and his well-being, especially at the moment, but it was obvious that Veronica shared at least some of his fascination. She would not be happy to know that I had allowed some wild, murderous creature to beat him to a pulp.

By the time I drew near to the vampire's glen, I'd resigned myself to saving him all over again, if necessary. I wasn't looking forward to dragging him miles through the inhospitable wilderness, or to the verbal lashing that was sure to follow once he regained consciousness, but I owed it to Veronica to try and tend to the things she cared about, including him.

Orion was lucky she liked him so much. For more reasons than he realized.

But then, he wasn't anywhere to be found, and I wondered if his safety was already a moot point. Maybe I'd find him in pieces and have to bring him back to the house in a box. *Can vampires regrow if you plant them in their coffins one limb at a time?*

The only thing I could see from my vantage point was a trail of destruction carved through the trees, denoting a very specific pathway through the woods. Whole trunks had been split and scarred. I followed in the wake of obvious catastrophe, keeping an eye out for anything unusual, such as a bloodless, disembodied leg. If Orion managed to get himself wounded again, I doubted he could have made it very far.

Inexplicably, nothing stood out, even from the air. Half a mile past the far edge of the wrecked grove, I landed amid a broken tangle of trampled grass and splintered wood. The smell of churned earth lingered richly in the air. I could see remnants of supernatural energy splashed across the path in front of me. *Like blood,* I thought, *but probably worse.*

The path continued for another hundred yards or so, weaving and narrowing. I tracked the energy traces to the base of what looked to be the oldest tree in the forest. Thick, gnarled roots spidered out from a towering trunk. The branches threatened to blot out the last of the sun.

But the tree's sheer natural majesty wasn't what drew my attention the most. There was a space hollowed out where the roots began their spread. It didn't seem large enough to accommodate a creature of the size of the one fighting with Orion. And yet, into that dusky cavern was where the trail of energy led.

Not to be deterred, no matter how the situation appeared, I gritted my teeth and entered the low, earthy passage. Despite my misgivings, the passage proved to be easily as tall as a man, and it only widened the farther I traveled. By the time I noticed a sweetly rotten smell of decay seeping into the air, it was much too late to turn back. My footsteps uncovered glints of bone mixed in with the soil, fragments of skull, loose teeth.

None of these were great signs, as far as how much I could expect to enjoy whatever I'd find at the end of the hidden path. I knew before I got there that I was walking uninvited into some kind of lair. My only saving grace was the creature's grave condition, as indicated by the trail it left. I read the energy patterns like blood spatter at a crime scene.

Maybe this thing was breathing its last. Maybe it was already dead.

The path took a sharp turn, hooking around suddenly into the mouth of a cavernous, dark chamber. The stench of death invaded my senses. Piles of bones had been heaped all around, including a precarious monolith made entirely of skulls. Where there had been remarkably little blood up to this point, the floor of the large cavern was stained with it.

I peered forward into the depth of the cave's shadows. It was there, barely visible as a grotesque silhouette against some sourceless, ambient glow. The bestial head was bowed, antlers scraping the ground. For a moment I thought it might really have died after all, until I saw the thin glow still burning in its eye sockets.

The creature made no move to attack me, and as I approached, I understood why. Although it might technically have emerged victorious from its most recent spate of battles, it did not escape unscathed. Most notable was the gaping hole torn in its ribcage, through which blood and various innards continually threatened to spill.

"You're dying," I said quietly. The lair's still, stagnant air clung to each word. I was met with no denial, and no submission, either. The eyes watched me, full of suspicion and wounded rage. I stepped closer to the shattered husk lying in its final repose. Slowly, the energy that fed its vengeful spirit leaked out, drifted away. "Is this what you want?"

The question was mostly rhetorical. No creature of such pure hate and hunger ever *wanted* to die. It was driven by the power of its need. But that power could no longer sustain a failing body on its own.

I reached out my hand and placed it on the splintered ribcage so that I could feel its life force. In the same moment, I learned what to call this armature of bones and blood, this vessel of death.

"Wendigo." The uttering of its name seemed to buy me a certain level of grudging respect. I guessed it must have been a little-known fact, not high in the priorities of the monster's victims. "You don't have much time left," I told it now. "But you know that."

The wendigo grunted. Nestled among the broken ribs, its heart pulsated rapidly. Had I the inclination, I could have plunged my hand down and grabbed it, ripped it out of its web of veins and arteries. The thought was tempting in a cruelly merciful way. I had another idea forming at the back of my mind, though—one that could benefit us both.

What do you want, fallen one? The wendigo's voice resonated through my whole body, but its strength was waning. I could feel it slipping toward the edge of the veil between realms. *Have you come to mock me?*

"No." I met its hollow gaze. "I can help you. In exchange for a favor."

The wendigo stared into my face. *Is that a bargain you are permitted to make?* The question held a tinge of ironic amusement. I wondered if perhaps I was underestimating the creature's capabilities. A voice in the back of my mind warned to tread lightly.

"It's what I'm offering," I said. "There's trouble brewing on the horizon. A tide that may never ebb if we let it come in." I was referring mostly to the enduring threat of invaders from the south, but Orion's plans for Veronica tumbled around in my thoughts as well. Did I want to turn the full-fledged wrath of a restored wendigo upon him? Not particularly.

But there were things about Veronica I did not think he understood. Things that could spell disaster if he tried to claim her as one of his own. And it wouldn't hurt to have a hidden ace up my sleeve, just in case.

What will you give me in exchange for my aid? Even inches from permanent death, the wendigo eked out a deal. I didn't like the cunning resourcefulness lurking behind its words, nor the gleam in its dead eyes.

"Life." I shrugged. "That's all you need."

Hmm. The wendigo glanced away, pretending to think. As if it wasn't backed into the tightest possible corner, teetering on the razor's edge between existence and oblivion. I waited patiently, sure of the answer that was to come. A minute later, it turned back to me. *Fine. Consider these terms accepted.*

"Promise," I said. "You'll be there when we call."

I see little choice for me, the wendigo admitted. *For once, you are the one who wields the power.* It paused. *I will answer your beckoning, fallen one. But yours alone.*

I could work with that. "Then I'll uphold my end of the deal. This might hurt."

The wendigo scoffed. *Pain is fleeting.*

I knelt down, resting both palms on patches of exposed bone. The wendigo lay still, heartbeat and breathing irregular, shallow. Hauling it back from the brink would not be as simple as it had been with Orion—every second drew it closer and closer to the void.

There was no more time to waste. I closed my eyes, filled my lungs with the dank, rotten air of the cave, and settled in to the task at hand.

$\mathcal{L}$ ian and Trent blocked me in the front hall. Just looking at them, I saw that my luck— and their patience—had run out. Trent, in particular, had the kind of steely glint in his eye that I usually reserved for whomever I happened to be hunting. I did not enjoy being on the receiving end of that look, but I was also aware that it might be something I deserved.

"You better start talking, V," he warned. "And you better have a real good explanation for whatever the fuck we just saw out there, because I know what it seemed like to me, and it's not great."

I glanced at Lian. Under normal circumstances, she might have been quick to jump to my defense, but not this time. That was when I knew for sure that I'd really fucked up. She stared at me, her dark eyes somber.

"I asked you to tell me the truth, V. Correct me if I'm wrong, but that's not what happened, is it?"

The entire confrontation reeked of a rebellious teen getting caught in our current situation. *We're not mad. We're disappointed.* Except that no, Trent was definitely super mad. I was ninety percent sure he wouldn't fight me in front of his ex-girlfriend, but that rogue ten percent had me bracing for a surprise attack.

"Okay, look." I ran both hands through my hair and sighed deeply. "I'm sorry. I messed up. I thought…well, who the hell knows what I thought. But it was obviously not the right decision. If I come clean now, will you forgive me?"

Lian grimaced. She put her hand on Trent's arm. "Give her a chance. Only one, though." Reluctantly, Trent stepped back to let me cross through into the living room. It had been a long time since I'd seen him so willing to let Lian take the lead. For months after Dylan's death, he'd been way too overprotective of her, too scared to let her have agency in a world cruel enough to murder his best friend.

It was nice to see some of the balance being restored between them. Even if it meant they were teaming up against me.

I sat down on one side of the coffee table in front of the dormant fireplace. Lian sat opposite me, and Trent stayed standing. He said nothing more, but he didn't have to. The storm clouds gathering in his eyes told me everything about where I stood with him. Namely, on ice thinner than a sheet of paper. One false move, and I'd plunge straight through.

"Where do you want me to start?" I asked. It seemed prudent to let them steer the conversation as they saw fit; I was the one doing wrong, and so I deserved no power. My hope was that deferring to their moral authority might earn back some of the friendship, loyalty, and integrity I had so recently hemorrhaged.

"The beginning." Lian crossed her legs and leaned back on the sofa cushions. She arched her eyebrows. "Wherever that is." I had never blamed Trent for being so into her he couldn't extricate himself if he tried, and right then, it was apparent exactly why. My sweet, gentle, sometimes overly-accommodating friend had been replaced by some no-nonsense ice queen. All the time she'd set aside for my bullshit was up.

"Don't kill me," I began, "but he and I are… involved. With each other."

She furrowed her brow. Standing beside the couch, Trent let out an annoyed growl.

"Seriously, V?" he demanded. "You can't be for real with this."

I pressed my lips together into a thin, tight line. "Sorry. It just kind of happened."

"Wh—" Briefly, Trent looked like he was seconds from lunging across the table at me. His expression blazed with incredulous contempt. But Lian held up her hand, a gesture that demanded tempers be held. He receded into simmering anger, his gaze still locked on me.

"Stuff like that doesn't just *happen*," Lian said. "I know you're not naïve enough to assume we're going to accept that."

"I'm serious," I insisted. "We met in passing one night while I was downtown. I didn't have any intention of doing anything or going anywhere with him. Our paths kept crossing until…" I shrugged. "I gave in."

Lian frowned at me. "So you're saying this all happened because you were thirsty."

"Well, when you put it like that, it starts to sound pretty shitty." I'd meant it as a joke, but nobody laughed. Not even me.

Trent shook his head. I could tell he was struggling to wrap his mind around the kind of debauchery to which I'd just admitted. "You've been fraternizing with the goddamn enemy the entire time," he muttered. "Un-fucking-believable."

"Hey, credit where credit is due," I shot back. "It hasn't been the whole time. I didn't come here with an ulterior motive."

"You just came up with one all by yourself." He made no effort to hide the disgust in his voice. "What else are you hiding, Veronica? Don't bother denying it. Secrets are like roaches in this line of work; where there's one, there's bound to be a thousand more hiding in the dark." I didn't answer him right away, so he went on, unable to stop himself. "I can't believe you can even say Dylan's name while you're jumping in bed with a vamp!"

That one stung. I winced, and Lian saw.

"Trent." She looked at him. "That's enough. Cool it or leave."

He hesitated, annoyance momentarily large on his face. All three of us understood a line had been crossed, and I had no doubt he was sorry for it. But his anger wouldn't subside long enough for an apology to surface. He left the room without another word. I expected the door to slam shut behind him. It didn't.

"He shouldn't have said that." Lian rubbed a hand across her face. "But I can't blame him for being pissed, V. And I don't think you can, either."

"No," I admitted. "It's fucked up. But I couldn't help it." *I still can't,* I thought, wisely choosing not to say that last part out loud. "I'm so sorry, Li. All you have to do is say the word, and I'll be on the next plane back to Seattle. Paying my own way."

She stared past me, lost in her own thoughts. Finally, she said, "I want to trust you, V. I really do. You've been an amazing friend to me for so long, and I don't want to lose that. But I don't get this shit at all. Like seriously, explain to me what the hell you think you're doing, all wrapped up with a vamp. You know as well as Trent does what they're like."

I wished I had a better explanation than the number of orgasms Orion reliably gave me. Not to mention that I hadn't said a thing about Seth or Logan. "It's just…this weird allure. I can't resist it. Doesn't cancel out how unappealing and douchey he can definitely be, but it keeps me coming back regardless." I paused. "Also, Trent was right. There's more."

"Oh, God." Lian held her head in her hands. "Why would you *do* this to me, V? Why would you do it to yourself? There's no benefit other than making your life a hundred times more complicated."

"Trust me, I'm fully aware. The longer we spend having this conversation, the more I'm asking the same questions." Detailing my actions out loud really brought the insanity into full relief. Was I playing the long game somehow? Or was I just a fucking idiot? I knew what Trent would say. "He's got friends. And I've been with them, too."

Lian's eyes widened in morbidly fascinated horror. "Please do not tell me that's why you went to the clan meeting," she pleaded. "My heart couldn't take it."

"What?" I made a face. "No. Oh my God, no. Let's just say Orion is a very rare exception to the general rule. The other one isn't a vamp." I wasn't sure why I decided last minute to only mention one of the remaining two. Maybe it made me seem less like I was having some kind of psychotic break.

"That's…good?" Lian was not optimistic.

"He's a demon," I said. "Like, from Hell."

"Veronica!" Her jaw dropped. "I mean, actually, that's a little bit hilarious. But I'm still mad at you, and having sex with the spawn of Satan as well as a vampire is still the worst idea you've ever had."

"To be fair, I have no idea who his dad is." I smiled slightly. "But yeah, it hasn't worked out so great. They don't really get along."

She groaned. "Of course they don't. Do you realize how crazy this is, V? Look me in the eye and tell me you know what a shit show you're putting on here."

"It's a hot mess," I agreed. "I have no idea how I'm going to clean it up."

Lian let out her breath. She closed her eyes for a moment or two, probably thinking about what to tell Trent so that she wouldn't have to lie, but he wouldn't end up out for my blood. "Can I ask you something?"

"Shoot. I'm an open book." All except for Logan. He had become my last dirty little secret, and I couldn't even explain the compulsion to keep him to myself.

"Has this thing with the vampire changed your perspective at all?" She examined me keenly. "As in, do you feel like you understand him?"

I laughed. "Oh, hell no. I'm in it for the sex. Nothing else."

She hesitated. "Don't tell Trent I asked you this, but is it really that good?"

I made eye contact with her and nodded slowly. "I promise I wouldn't be within ten feet of him if it wasn't."

She snorted. "I'm gonna call the Grand and ask them to shut off all the hot water to your room. Cold showers only from now on, 'cause apparently you need them."

I'd graduated from telling full lies to half-truths. It was true that I craved sex with Orion on a shamefully frequent basis. But despite my insistence to the contrary, both to Lian and to myself, I kind of liked him too. He was charming, in an arrogant, exasperating way. And even though I hated his unyielding jealousy, I liked the feeling of being wanted so much.

Didn't tell her that, though. I just chuckled and said, "It's a little late for that."

Lian leaned forward and held out her hand. "Truce? I hate fighting with you, V. Honestly."

I smiled and took her hand in mine. "Truce. I know you do, and I'm sorry. This one's all on me."

She squeezed my hand. Then she got up, came

around the table, and hugged me tightly. "I can't promise much as far as Trent's concerned, but I'll work on him, okay? I think he'll come around eventually."

"Thanks. Let him have all the time he needs. He's got every right to be furious."

"I'll tell him you said so." Lian gave my hand another squeeze. She smiled before she left. I felt like the biggest weight in the world had been lifted from my chest as I walked back to my room.

That relief lasted until the sound of knocking came at the window less than five minutes later. The curtain was drawn, but I could see the shadow of a figure waiting on the other side of the glass. When I pushed the curtain back, Seth's golden eyes burned into mine.

Against my better judgment, I opened the window. How was it that these damn supernatural men managed to subvert my convictions so easily? I knew it was a bad choice, and yet it was so easy to let him in.

"What are you doing here?" I asked.

He kissed me hotly. "You owe me. And I've got a pretty good idea about how I want to collect."

The rational voice in my head screamed at me

to tell him no, to kick him right back out that window. It wasn't loud enough to override the intense heat washing through my body.

I stared at his chiseled, sharply handsome features and said, "Okay."

CHAPTER 22

SETH

She was my first real taste of life back on this side of the veil, which was exactly how I wanted it. The soft, human warmth of her skin was almost like a drug to me. I drank her in, every part of her. The more I touched and tasted, the faster her heart beat, blood rushing through her veins.

Turning her on was a game. Not a difficult one, but I needed to win.

She let me take her shirt off before she realized that what we were about to do might not work out well for her. I knew there were other people in the house—I could feel their energy through the walls and the floor. I just didn't care.

"Wait." Veronica stopped me with her hands on

my chest. She tossed her hair back, out of her eyes, and stared at me in what she must have thought was a serious, no-nonsense way. "We can't do this right now."

"Little late for that." I bent my head and kissed each of her rosy nipples. They stiffened against my mouth. Fuck I'd missed her so much. "Your body agrees."

She sucked in a sharp breath. "I mean it, Seth. Now is not the time or place."

I glanced up from between her breasts. "I hate to break it to you gorgeous, but it never will be. You're not exactly dealing with the kid next door here."

"Ugh." Veronica rolled her eyes. She pushed me backward toward the foot of the bed. "You have to go. This is my friend's house." Her gaze darted to the door. "She's home. And so is Trent." When she spoke the guy's name, her voice dropped to just above a whisper.

"So what? You got a thing for him?" Undeterred, I gave her another kiss.

"No!" She squirmed unconvincingly. "But if they catch us, we're probably both dead. Trent already saw Orion. He'd kill you without a second look."

"Huh." The threat of danger only added an edge to the fire already burning in me. I pushed her back on the pillows. "Then you'd better be quiet."

She was pissed at me for sure, but the slayer didn't put up much more of a fight. She writhed in ecstasy as I tasted her deeper, one hand clamped over her mouth, I made my way down her body, kissing her over clothes as my hand tugged up at her skirt. Every so often, a moan or a squeal would make it through her fingers. I gripped her quivering thighs, pushed aside her underwear, and plunged my tongue as far as I could. She smelled delicious and I lost myself to her, remembering why I couldn't get her out of my mind, why the fuck I needed her so insatiably.

Veronica grunted. She pressed her pelvis into my mouth. I sucked her; she yelped, and then she whispered, "Oh, fuck." And without giving her time to breathe, I changed positions. Up on my feet, I grabbed her gorgeous hips and spun her over onto her stomach, then dragged them back toward me. Kneeling forward, she stuck that gorgeous ass into the air, while I pushed her skirt out of the way, along with her thong.

If there was anything I had missed the most about the mortal realm, it was the tight, muscular softness that gripped me as I entered her slick warmth, and continued to grab at me with every following thrust. I rode her from behind, watching her slender back buck and flex. Her hands clenched into tight fists in the sheets. As she climbed toward orgasm, she seized a pillow and bit into it, hard.

"Come on, baby." I pounded into her. "Let it out. I know you want to."

Every muscle in Veronica's perfect body flexed. The force of her pleasure nearly knocked her out, drawing my own explosion. I hissed, pumping into her. Even her toes curled as she dove down into the mattress, I heard a long, muffled moan. Her hips gyrated hungrily on their own, drawing out every last sensation while I floated on ecstasy.

Something about the way she lay limply in the aftermath, half wrapped in the tangle we'd made of the covers, convinced me to stay by her side. Her eyes were closed, and she looked like a piece of art, even with her tousled hair and sweat gleaming on her skin.

"Goddammit," she muttered. Despite her efforts at low volume, her voice was still slightly hoarse. "I kind of hate you."

"Oh yeah?" I stretched out casually beside her. "Could have fooled me just now."

Veronica rolled over to face me. She ran her index finger up my arm, over my shoulder, and along the side of my neck. As if by some unseen magnetism, her body wrapped itself gently around mine, so that her cheek ended up nestled against my chest, our legs entwined.

"I know you're so warm because you're from Hell, and I really shouldn't be okay with that. And yet, here we are."

I smirked. "This from the woman who wanted me to leave half an hour ago."

"Consider me persuaded," she replied sleepily. Her fingers traced restless patterns on my skin. "Are you gonna tell me where you've been this whole time? Or are you just going to leave me hanging forever?"

"I'm surprised you're interested," I told her. "It's not really the concern of mortals where people like me end up after we get screwed."

"Why wouldn't I be?" She tilted her head to make eye contact. "First of all, I was having those crazy dreams, and I know it was you in them. Second…" She trailed off and shrugged her shoulders. "I guess I was worried about you."

When was the last time I'd ever heard anyone say that about me, let alone a girl like her? Mildly disturbed by the warm contentment suddenly kindling in my heart region, I squashed it down. "That was a waste of your time and energy, but I appreciate the sentiment."

She chuckled. "You're welcome."

We lay there in silence for a few minutes while I tried to figure out how to explain everything I'd been through over the past however long it had been. "There's…" I paused, shook my head, and tried again. "There are some places in this realm where the walls are thin. And sometimes you can make doorways in them and pass between places. I was, uh…on the other side of a door."

"But you could see me through it. And I could see you, sometimes."

"Only while you were asleep," I said. "Mortals usually can't see shit, even if they really try. Don't ask me why that is. You're just inferior that way."

She frowned a little. "I'm a slayer, though. That elevates me somewhat, doesn't it?"

I stroked her tender, fragile skin, feeling all the vitality just barely contained underneath. It would have been so easy to pierce that layer immediately and watch her life drain faster than she could slow it.

"Maybe… not sure," I said. I didn't add that it was one of the things I liked about her.

She kissed my neck. "It's still good to have you back. Does that mean you found a door that was open and were able to walk through?"

"Sort of." I remembered the mirrors, and the howl of agony that had sounded at the moment I broke through. "Let's just say I made my own."

She sighed. "For the sake of us both, I'm choosing to ignore that."

A new silence fell, one that lasted for a long time. She lay perfectly still, and I was beginning to think she'd fallen asleep. And then she shifted her weight and spoke up. "Okay, I need to ask you something."

"I don't need to answer, but you can try."

"Don't be mad," she said. It was such a strange, vulnerable response that I looked at her, trying to read her face. Veronica did not return my gaze. "Is Orion all right?"

Suddenly, I understood why she'd led with that particular stipulation. It was remarkable how quickly the mention of one individual could sour the mood. I took my arm from around her and sat up, putting some distance between us. She stayed where she was.

"As far as I know, he's going to be fine," was what I told her. The truth was, I had no idea what was happening to him as we spoke. My limited understanding told me that his stupid coffin ought to fix everything. But if there was a ritual involved, I sure hadn't done it.

"Okay." She took a breath in and let it out. "Thank you. For all your help."

"It wasn't much, to be honest with you." Against all reason, I felt my anger melting away. She had an effect I didn't understand. I could count on one hand the number of times I'd been soothed in my life. But I let her kiss me.

"It was enough," she said and smiled.

I stared at her. *When the fuck did I get to be such a goddamn sucker?*

She only gave me a little while longer to wonder. "Look, I'm sorry to kick you out so soon, but you really need to go now." She looked at the door. "They think I'm hurt, and they're going to check on me at some point. I know you think you're invincible, but I'm willing to bet Trent will want to prove you wrong."

"He'd fail, but I get what you're saying." Besides,

she was right. I was already getting dangerously close to overstaying my welcome, if there was one to begin with. Trent, whoever he was, had been pissed from the moment I arrived, and his temper showed no signs of changing. I recognized that simmering cauldron of emotion; it was the same one I'd managed to put a lid on a few minutes earlier.

"That attitude is going to bite you in the ass someday," Veronica warned. She stole one more kiss as she pushed me toward the window.

I winked at her. "Maybe I'm into that."

If she replied, I didn't hear it. The outside air came with a refreshing sense of freedom so powerful that I wondered why the fuck I'd lingered so long in that damn house anyway. But then I looked over my shoulder at the room she was in—and I knew exactly why.

Because she was in there. And apparently, she was becoming a good reason for a lot of things.

CHAPTER 23
LOGAN

Having existed for so long in parallel with death itself, there was not much left in the mortal realm that could faze me—except the act of reviving another death spirit. As I worked to restore the wendigo, I could feel its energy trying to latch on to mine and drag me down into the strange purgatory where it lingered. Even in its dire state, it retained its eternal hunger.

There were a hundred moments during that struggle where I had the opportunity to pause and rethink the actions I had decided to take. If I had known, or tried harder to anticipate what could come of bringing a vengeful, devouring spirit back into the mortal realm, maybe I would've backed away before the process was complete.

But I was too focused on the way in which a perpetually starving wendigo could be geared toward becoming the solution to our looming problem. The Seattle clan wasn't going to wait forever to make their return, especially not once they found out the sheer numbers Orion had lost. We needed some kind of reinforcement as soon as we could get it.

And we were nothing if not beggars at this point, which meant being choosers was out of the question.

I came out of the revival with my head spinning, tendrils of nausea wrapped around my stomach. For a mercifully peaceful moment, I closed my eyes and breathed in—until the fetid odor in the air reminded me where I was.

"I need to get out of here," I muttered. Stumbling to my feet, I caught the briefest glimpse of the wendigo watching me. The glow in its deep black eye sockets was steady now, its bones no longer brittle and on the verge of breaking.

Now you flee, fallen one? Tempering your compassion with cowardice?

I shook my head. "No, I might—" Somehow, it felt wrong to inform a mystical being such as this, no matter how terrible, that I was about to throw up, so I just shut my mouth and went for the exit. Fortunately, the wendigo seemed to understand. Minutes after I had finally emerged into the gray dregs of daylight and the freshest air I'd ever smelled, it came out of its lair behind me.

I bent over with my hands on my knees. The scent of the forest washed through my nose and mouth, cleansing my body of the lair's foulness. I knelt, and then sat on the damp ground. Never had I been so thankful to simply exist in a different space.

"Don't forget the deal we made," I told the wendigo at length, once I was reasonably sure the sickness had ebbed. "I'll hold you to it."

The wendigo hunkered down onto its skeletal haunches. It looked much more bestial that way, less like a being capable of the kind of thought it displayed. I examined it carefully from where I sat. Despite my commitment to diplomacy for the sake of securing its aid in the future, I couldn't shake the feeling of sizing up a foe.

I will remember, it said.

Which left me to ponder the worth of a monster's promise as I stood up and got ready to leave. I'd half expected the wendigo to depart before me, but it obviously wasn't comfortable leaving me alone at the mouth of its den. I thought about trying to reassure it that I had no desire at all to revisit that location, then decided it didn't matter. My goals had been accomplished, and it was time to go.

For all I knew, Orion could be moldering in the earth somewhere, or wandering around an especially remote section of the forest, incapacitated by his injuries. Now that the wendigo was more or less taken care of, new and larger challenges rose up before me.

"Be safe," I told the wendigo. "I wasn't lying when I said we'll need you." Our alliance was new and tenuous, but it was there nonetheless.

The creature bowed its head, great, jagged antlers sweeping over the dirt. We locked gazes. I could sense its mind reaching out in the same way a mouth must be opened in order to speak.

Wait. The single word was followed by a long, pregnant pause. I wondered what the wendigo's depth of understanding really was. It knew enough to speak in grave platitudes and taunt me rather gracefully, but how much did it actually think?

As I found out, it had been thinking entirely too much.

"The deal has been struck," I said calmly. "If you want to change the terms, be ready to pay."

The wendigo continued as if I hadn't spoken at all. *I have a question.*

I raised an eyebrow. "Go on."

Slowly, the wendigo's whole body turned. Even healed, it wasn't much of a thing to behold, as far as beauty was concerned. The exposed teeth in its jaw grinned at me, starkly contrasting the rest of its expressionless features.

Who is she?

That was when I knew for sure that I'd probably made an incredible mistake. Temporarily frozen, I wracked my brain for an answer that might satisfy the creature without damning Veronica to a lifetime as the object of its twisted fascination. Orion's burning interest was passing in comparison. She would never be free of this thing, in life or in death.

"She is none of your concern." I kept my voice civil, though a few degrees cooler. "That is a fact. Not an opinion."

She is human. The wendigo tilted its head, bemused. *And she is not. Her spirit...* It trailed off, most likely imagining how it might feel to consume both flesh and soul of a slayer. I couldn't read its face, but whatever crumb of trust I harbored was long gone.

"Let me make something very clear." I stepped forward to emphasize my point. Directly into its line of sight. The baleful glowing eyes focused raptly on me. A stare full of ravenous hunger. "Do not touch her. If you harm her in any way, I will slaughter you, and we will find another way to deal with our problems." Orion's clan was in dire straits, but not so dire that I was willing to sacrifice Veronica.

It was a rare point on which I knew he and I agreed.

She is special. The wendigo nodded slightly. Some type of base recognition registered in that macabre face—how, I could not explain. *I see.*

"You could say that." I squared my stance. "There will be no escape from wrath should you pursue her." For the first time, the unspoken rivalry that had erupted between Orion, Seth, and me served a useful purpose. I was reasonably confident in our ability to unite, as long as Veronica might be at stake.

Still, it couldn't be anything but a worst-case scenario. Just imagining Orion's dramatics clashing with Seth's unbridled rage was enough to make my stomach turn again.

You would hunt me. The wendigo lifted its head, casting me in deep shadow.

"Not only that," I affirmed. "We would kill you. For good." Whether or not such a thing was truly possible, I wasn't sure. But I knew now that there was a place for things like wendigo spirits to go. And if it was anything like Seth's little Underworld vacation, it wouldn't be very pleasant.

The wendigo hesitated. It glanced off into the deep, dark forest, as if listening to sounds no one else could hear. The wind whistled softly through the gaps between its bones, playing a lonely, haunting song. How many souls had this beast trapped in its grasp? Were they not able to sate its appetite?

I knew the answer already, that a creature like the wendigo would never be full. And now I harbored an awful, nagging suspicion that all I'd really done was place Veronica squarely in its sights.

"Wendigo." I spoke its name sharply, with the sort of icy authority learned in the world of the fallen. It glanced back, startled. "Swear to me. The girl is not yours."

I understand your words, it answered. We stared at each other in defiant silence. The trickles of light filtering down through the trees had turned milky and silver, an indication that once I cleared the canopy, I'd be flying in the eye of the moon.

I thought perhaps the creature had more to say, but I was wrong. After a protracted stalemate, it finally turned and loped off. The way its whole grotesque form disappeared into the shadows was as impressive as it was unnerving. Where there should have been crashing through brush and tree branches, there was absolutely nothing.

I didn't like it.

Silver streaked the jet-black treetops of Chugach as I let the updraft carry me higher. Even though the moon was nearing fullness, there wasn't much to see. The only traceable aspect of the wendigo was its pervasive aura of death. I focused in on the echo of its raw, bottomless craving and began to follow it through the wilderness.

And almost immediately, I could tell by the sharply honed precision of its trajectory that the wendigo was on the hunt. It was more or less invisible to me, except for its energy signature, and yet the farther we traveled, the lower my stomach continued to sink. There were a lot of things I did not appreciate about what was beginning to unfold, not least of which was the beeline it was making for a side of the park that faced roads leading into residential areas.

But it kept going, and soon it was too late to stop it even if I had intended to try. I saw its other-worldly shape transition from the cover of the forest into the ambient darkness of the night, making little effort to avoid the growing signs of civilization.

I grimaced. Wherever this thing was going with such single-minded determination, there'd be hell to pay once it arrived. Cruising over the silent streets on the outskirts of Anchorage, I prepared to witness another murder.

CHAPTER 24

ORION

The smell of earth drew me up from the bottom of a dreamless well, back toward the realm of the living and the mortal. I opened my eyes to the lid of my sarcophagus sitting askew, soil scattered all over the floor. When I made an attempt to stand, the whole apparatus teetered dangerously, spilling yet more soil across the floorboards.

It was all intensely sacrilegious. But right then, I lacked the capacity to care. My mind was disturbingly foggy, like the surface of an iced-over mirror. I knew, in theory, that things had happened—quite a lot of things, in fact. The details of those events eluded me by inches, skating just beyond my grasp.

But suddenly, the ice began to melt. Memories of the past few days came flooding back, and in an instant I understood everything—where I was, how I'd gotten there, and who was responsible for the dirt all over the floor. The answer wasn't as surprising as it was enraging. My first instinct was to find that fucking demon and send him straight back to the prison he'd escaped. It was the least he deserved, except I also understood he did it to save me. Even if it was in his own barbaric way.

And yet, the fact that Veronica had begged him to save me cooled my anger. Paradoxically, it bothered me that her persuasion worked so well; Seth obviously had a soft spot for her beyond his crass interest in her body. But knowing he'd acted solely upon her request was just enough to put me in a more rational state of mind.

He hadn't *just* dumped me into my resting place like so many pounds of meat. He'd done it because Veronica pleaded for my life. And he didn't know yet, but that one fact made him the luckiest demon on Earth—and the accompanying knowledge that Veronica was somewhere relatively safe.

Besides, I had much bigger things to worry about. Any leftover beef with Seth paled in comparison to the problems the Anchorage clan was facing. Our numbers had just suffered massive depletion due to an outside force I failed to predict. Standing there in the dim bedroom, it dawned on me that I didn't even have a solid grasp on how many were left.

For all I knew, Anchorage could be facing clan extinction. Which meant that once the Seattle faction showed up again, as was inevitable, there would be no one to fight them back. I was proud, but not delusional about my chances against an army of my enemies. As it stood, Anchorage was on the verge of becoming my nemesis' latest acquisition.

"I'd rather Seth let me die," I muttered darkly. On my way downstairs, I put out a summons as far as it would go, calling my wayward cohorts back to my side. If I had harbored any fleeting notions that perhaps Seth's return could be attributed to a particularly vivid bad dream, they were soon dispelled by his prompt response.

Get back to the house, was the order. *This is a clan emergency.*

Oh, so you are still alive. Yeah, yeah. I'm on my way.

Logan didn't answer directly, but I could sense him moving in the right direction. His trajectory—

heading from Chugach—confused me, but I didn't have time or space to worry about it at the moment. Waiting for them was agony on its own; by the time Seth showed up, I had migrated out to the front yard.

"Hey." He looked me up and down and did a decent job of hiding the smirk that threatened to jump across his lips. But his energy sliced through the air like a knife, carrying an unmistakable tinge of Veronica. I didn't have to speculate very hard to suspect the context of their meeting; not while he wore that smug grin on his face.

I glowered. "How was the Underworld? I have to say, I'm a little surprised you made it back so soon."

He chuckled. "Disappointed, you mean. You can say it." He paused. "And jealous, I would assume." Every word he said was dripping with bait, the kind meant to goad me into starting a fight. There was little I would've liked more than to wipe the floor with him, but doing so would only consume precious time and resources. And was it him I was furious at, or that I'd lost my entire following?

I clenched my teeth. "The clan is fucked, Seth. We can't stand up to Seattle like this."

"So I've seen," he answered easily.

I took a deep breath, nearly choking on my pride. "Did you happen to see how many survived?"

"What? The attack by that thing?" He spoke as if there was anything else I could possibly be talking about. "Hard to say. There might have been a handful who came out of it all right."

It was almost impossible to tell if he was lying. He stared me in the eyes, his expression inscrutable. Not a flicker of emotion showed through. I could've punched him, but restraint barely won out.

"I need to find them," I said, keeping my tone even. "And then I need to make more."

The ambiguous implication of violence piqued Seth's curiosity. He raised his eyebrows. I felt his attention sharpen by a few degrees. "I'm listening," he said briefly. "Tell me more."

Neither of us noticed Logan approach until he had been there for an indeterminate amount of time, just watching us. "The clan must enter a phase of recruitment," I was telling Seth. "It hasn't been necessary in quite some time, but I'm afraid it's unavoidable now." My mind flashed back to the days of mass turnings, legions of thralls. The recollections were bittersweet, to say the least.

So many of those once-loyal servants were lost. It stung, but I refused to let it affect me.

"Why do you sound hesitant?" the demon asked. He was blunt, and I resented his perceptiveness. "I thought you guys were all about expanding your empires or whatever." He gestured in Logan's direction. "I mean, we're here because you don't want some other asshole taking over your turf."

"The process is complicated." I ran my fingers through my hair. "It causes unrest. Sometimes it can take months for those waves to settle again. Sometimes it takes years."

"It can take centuries," Logan interjected. His voice was flat, but the look in his eyes was intensely focused. For some reason, his normally ghostly skin looked even paler under the moonlight, which threw his features into sharp relief.

Seth turned to observe him. "What happened? You sick?"

Logan shot the demon a withering glance. "No." To me, he said, "Please continue."

I cleared my throat. "Well, that is true. In rare cases, the ramifications of a blood moon can span generations." Whole vampire dynasties had risen and fallen around blood moons of the past. The entire face of a clan could be shaped, or changed, by the ways in which its population waxed and waned.

"A *blood moon?*" Seth grinned. "Holy shit. That's the most interesting thing you've ever said to me." A keen glow sparked in his eyes. "I'm pretty sure I can help make this happen. No matter what it is."

I grimaced. The blood moon was at once incredibly profane and sacred in a strange kind of way. In my younger years, I had treated the birth of each new vampire into my clan as a blessed occasion, a celebration. This time, there was no such luxury. It pained me to have to involve two outsiders in what was perhaps the most intimate aspect of the clan's culture. Indeed, I'd intended to save the experience to be shared between Veronica and me.

But the gravity of the situation simply couldn't be ignored. To Logan, I said, "Seth claims there were survivors of the wendigo attack. Go and find them, and help them hunt down mortals to turn. As many as you can."

"You sure you want to be letting just anyone with a pulse into your club?" Seth asked. "I know your standards aren't real high to begin with, but this seems like a risky proposition."

I glared in his direction. "Don't fucking argue. You're the security. If you meet resistance, crush it." I paused. "I'll convert half the damn city if I need to."

"That's it? They do what we say, or they die?" Seth was incredulous. I knew full well that I had just handed him a dangerous set of orders. Depending on how compliant the population of Anchorage decided to be tonight, I could expect to wake up to blood running in the streets—maybe literally. His lack of conscience was the precise reason he'd been hand-picked for the job he was about to do.

I hoped all the hassle would finally pay off.

Nodding, I said, "Desperate times call for desperate measures."

He laughed. His teeth gleamed. "Ain't that the truth. I'm just glad you're finally loosening the leash a little."

"Don't get used to it." I frowned. *Especially not where Veronica is concerned.* It wasn't my intention to bring her up at all, in an effort to keep things civil, but as he and Logan were turning to leave, the urge peaked, and I was unable to help myself. "Where is V, Seth? Is she still in that house?"

"I thought you'd never ask." He looked over his shoulder. "Yeah, she's there. Nice place. Two other people. One of them's a guy, and he's like her." He winked. "I did a little recon for you. You can thank me later."

I saw a flash of red. "Who the fuck is he?" Had she been with him, too? I decided that once we were finally reunited, Veronica and I were going to have a talk about boundaries. She was sorely mistaken if she thought I was willing to share her forever.

The moment she became my sweet little vampire thrall, she was mine only.

Seth shrugged. "No idea. But I don't think he's banging her. Or if he was, they're not doing it anymore. He was pissed off the whole time I was there."

Somehow, that offended me too. More and more questions kept cropping up in my brain, but the part of me that wasn't focused solely on Veronica made me let him go. Wordless, I waved the two of them off and stormed back into the house. For now, much as it pained me, I needed to leave Veronica and everything about her in the background.

She would be dealt with the moment the Anchorage clan was back on its feet. And to that end, I pledged to grow it as fast as possible, through any necessary means. Maybe it was time at last to let Seth live up to his full homicidal potential. For all of my hard feelings towards him, I had absolutely no doubt that he could prepare an army of thralls as easily as they could be turned.

If we did everything right, we could practically bounce back overnight. Not as strong and stable as we had been before the wendigo struck, but powerful enough at least to hold our own when the Seattle tide came crashing in again.

All we had to do was buy enough time. Even at rock bottom, I still held the city in the palm of my hand. It was simply a matter of bending it, slowly and surely, to my will. And when that was done, I'd retrace my steps to the house where my Veronica was being kept away.

Because I had every intention of taking back what was mine.

CHAPTER 25

VERONICA

*L*ong after Seth left, I could still feel him on me as I lay in the bed, mulling over the string of bad choices I continued to make. As much as I tried to live in blissful ignorance, it was becoming very clear that these men each affected me in the weirdest ways. All my rationality and good slayer sense, the very things in which I had once taken so much pride, went out the window as soon as they got close.

And it was becoming a problem. I hadn't meant to sleep with Seth, or catch feelings for Orion, or get wrapped up with Logan too, and yet I'd done all of those things with a goddamn smile on my face. Groaning, I rolled over away from the window, locking both arms around my pillow.

"Girl, you are the hottest mess," I muttered, my voice muffled and practically unintelligible. "Like, seriously. We need to get our shit together." I cringed into myself, thinking about what Lian might say if she knew I was banging a demon literal minutes after our heart-to-heart. Trent would probably just toss me out on my ear. He'd never had much tolerance for bullshit, and I knew I was testing his capacity.

The only thing saving me was the fact that we were in Lian's family home, and he was nothing if not respectful to her agency. They fought about things like the amount of time they spent together and her allegiances to dumbasses like me. Not about her strong will or her need for independence.

All of the things I understood Orion trying to snuff out in me, Trent encouraged in Lian. And once upon a time, his best friend Dylan had been like that too. I squeezed the pillow tighter and let out a heavy, wistful sigh. In an alternate universe, the four of us were still a team. Us against the world, like we always thought it would be forever.

But Dylan was gone, and I was up to my face in a situation so complicated it defied mortal imagining. It was so stupid I almost had to laugh about it.

Unfortunately, its stupidity didn't erase any of the very real feelings I had. To my disappointment, neither did my dirty little secret being out. I knew that my friends were pissed at me. It hurt.

Nonetheless, I allowed Seth to climb through that window. In my extremely weak defense, he hadn't given me a vast array of options, and I was not in a place to fight with him. My senses were still shot to hell; unsurprisingly, banging the shit out of a fire demon did not help. All I wanted to do now was curl up and sleep the rest of the night away. *Maybe things will be chill again when I wake up.*

But I couldn't get to sleep. I kept thinking about Logan and Orion, who had taken the place Seth previously occupied in my thoughts. It was kind of funny to imagine how mad Orion would be to know I'd seen him looking so bad, but I was also really worried. Even for a vampire clanmaster, he'd seemed to be inches from real, permanent death.

"I should have been more specific when I asked Seth to help him." For the first time, hours too late, I realized how crazy it was to beg Seth, of all people, to save Orion's life. Mortified, I covered my face. "They fucking hate each other!" How did I know Seth hadn't just dumped the body somewhere and come back to get laid?

I didn't. The trust I had in all of them was blind and foolish, but I couldn't help it. It was like they each filled a void in me that I wasn't aware of until they pointed it out with their presence. Logan especially carved out a tender place in my heart. He was too sad and gentle to carry the full hatred of which I knew Orion and Seth were capable.

Lying there in the calm dark of the bedroom, I closed my eyes and tried to stretch my senses, feeling for a response. Instead, I felt that the last twenty-four hours, or however many it had been, kicked my ass to Hell and back. Not even ten seconds into the attempt, a sharp, blinding pain sliced down behind my eye.

I sucked air in through clenched teeth. "Ah, fuck! Okay, okay, bad idea." As if scolding me, the stabbing in my eyeball remained as an echo after I eased off. Without my senses, there was no way to pinpoint exactly where the boys were. "I'm sure they're fine," I told myself, closing my eyes one more time. "They're strong. They're tough. They would want me to be resting right now."

Again, the thought, however true, failed to lull me down into the sleep I craved. The best I could manage was a light, fitful doze. Senseless half-dreams danced through my head. My spirit wanted to be with all three of them at once—I felt them pulling me in different directions. In those dreams, Orion was healthy, but pissed. He paced the yard of the house on the inlet, eyes dark, thoughts obviously racing.

I saw a glimpse of them together, Orion giving orders, Seth with that smug, cocky grin on his lips. The way he'd smiled at me as he came through the window. Floating in the purgatory of incorporeal space that's so frustratingly common in dreams, I strained to hear the words leaving their mouths.

"Is this real?" I wondered, half aloud and half in my mind. If it was, I received no answer. Neither vamp, nor demon, nor my strong and silent angel heard me.

Then, quite suddenly, my consciousness was jerked away to somewhere else. The field of view was under constant motion, and the images I was seeing looked strange. There were no bright colors, only varying tones of black and gray. The effect disoriented me completely at first; the struggle was so intense that it woke me up.

"What the…" I rubbed my eyes and sat up in the bed. "That was *so* weird." What I wanted was to wake up and get ready to jump back in the fray, because clearly the whole recuperation thing wasn't working out that well. I needed to be active, to be working in the field. All this time in bed was wreaking havoc on my brain.

It might be hard to get going at first, but I was down to risk it, confident my body would catch up soon. *Just don't take any insane risks for a while. It'll be fine.*

No matter how willing the spirit was, the flesh continued to refuse cooperation. The odd lure of that last dream pulled me back toward comfortable semi-consciousness. *You're not ready, V,* whispered a little voice in my ear. *You'll get your shit kicked in if you try getting out there right now. Just lean back, shut your eyes, and let the boys handle it.*

I wasn't convinced, but the energy would not be mustered. Before I knew what was happening, I had eased back down onto the pillows and was drifting off against my own will.

The moving grayscale images returned. They shifted left and right, as if looking around, and I was startled to find that I recognized the surroundings. My heart flipped sickeningly in my chest as I bounded across familiar wide, manicured lawns, passing through the shadows of huge, far-apart homes.

"What the hell," I whispered. "I think this is—"

Moments later, I broke through a line of trees, and all my suspicions were instantly proven. Lian's house stood less than a hundred feet away, and the distance kept closing. The second floor windows drew closer and closer, and I realized how unnaturally tall I was. Through the glass, I saw a bed, and a person lying on it.

My eyes snapped open. I bolted upright so fast the room spun. Still in bed, I spun to face the window, just in time to see the looming, grotesquely skeletal silhouette of the wendigo filling the frame. Its hand, long fingers outstretched, smashed through splintering glass and wood, reaching for me.

I stared. Time slowed to a crawl. I had enough time to see and understand exactly what was taking place, but not enough to escape. The wendigo wasn't hurt anymore; in my current state, I was no match for its speed and strength.

I remember a scream hit my ears as it dragged me over the jagged remnants of the window. It was only later that I realized that shrill, terror-driven sound had come from me. I thrashed in the wendigo's grasp, kicking and pounding with every last ounce of my energy.

The monster could not have cared less. It

changed directions and swung me around, and right before it took off running, I got one final brief look into Lian's guest room just as the door came crashing in.

"Veronica!" Lian beat Trent to the window. She leaned out, and the last thing I saw was her face, frozen into a mask of horror and fear. *"Veronica!"*

Continue Chosen Vampire Series. Click here to grab book 3, Blood Kissed.

KEEP
CALM
AND
CARRY
GARLIC

Making a deal with a vampire, demon and fallen angel were never part of my plan, and neither was being claimed by them.

SAVAGE SECTOR

NEW SHADOWLANDS SERIES

Being rejected by my fated mate is the least of my problems...

I'm a half-breed, a Cursed. The wolf half gets me an alpha for a fated mate...the witch half gets me killed.

Or so they think.

Now four Viking Alphas are all that stand between me and certain death. They need my powers to take over the Savage Sector, and they'll hold my sisters' as leverage until they get what they want from me.

My wild magic, my heart.

My wolf calls to them, but I can't trust them to keep me alive once this is over.

I'm just an Omega to them, but that mistake may cost us all our lives

What the Viking Alphas want, the Viking Alphas get...

...and right now that's me and my wild magic.

Savage Sector is set in the same world as Shadowlands Sector, with some cross over of characters. It can be read without having read Shadowlands first.

Shadowlands

Shadowlands Sector, One

Shadowlands Sector, Two

Shadowlands Sector, Three

Chosen Vampire Slayer

Night Kissed

Moon Kissed

Blood Kissed

Winter's Thorn

To Seduce A Fae

To Tame A Fae

To Claim A Fae

Shadow Hunters Series

Boxed Set 1

Wicked Heat Series

Wicked Heat #1

Wicked Heat #2

Wicked Heat #3

Elemental Series

Taking Breath #1

Taking Breath #2

Gods and Monsters

Apollo Is Mine

Poseidon Is Mine

Ares Is Mine

Hades Is Mine

Haven Realm Series

Hunted (Little Red Riding Hood Retelling)

Cursed (Beauty and the Beast Retelling)

Entangled (Rapunzel Retelling)

Princess of Frost (Snow Queen)

Kingdom of Wolves Co-write with C.R. Jane

Wild Moon

Playing with Hellfire Co-write with Harper A. Brooks

Playing with Hellfire

Hell in a Handbasket

Thief of Hearts Series Co-write with C.R. Jane

Siren Condemned

Siren Sacrificed

Siren Awakened

Broken Souls Series Co-write with C.R. Jane

School of Broken Souls

School of Broken Hearts

School of Broken Dreams

School of Broken Wings

Fallen World Series Co-write with C.R. Jane

Bound

Broken

Betrayed

Belong

Beautiful Beasts Academy Co-write with Kim Faulks

Manicures and Mayhem

Diamonds and Demons

Hexes and Hounds

Secrets and Shadows

Passions and Protectors

Ancients and Anarchy

milayoungarc@gmail.com